Marriage à la Mode

by

Elisabeth Fairchild

A SIGNET BOOK

SIGNET
Published by the Penguin Group
Penguin Putnam Inc., 375 Hudson Street,
New York, New York 10014, U.S.A.
Penguin Books Ltd, 27 Wrights Lane,
London W8 5TZ, England
Penguin Books Australia Ltd, Ringwood,
Victoria, Australia
Penguin Books Canada Ltd, 10 Alcorn Avenue,
Toronto, Ontario, Canada M4V 3B2
Penguin Books (N.Z.) Ltd, 182–190 Wairau Road,
Auckland 10, New Zealand

Penguin Books Ltd, Registered Offices:
Harmondsworth, Middlesex, England

First published by Signet, an imprint of Dutton Signet,
a member of Penguin Putnam Inc.

First Printing, December, 1997
10 9 8 7 6 5 4 3 2 1

 REGISTERED TRADEMARK—MARCA REGISTRADA

Printed in the United States of America

SIGNET REGENCY ROMANCE
Coming in January 1998

Andrea Pickens
The Defiant Governess

Nancy Butler
Lord Monteith's Gift

Eileen Putman
The Dastardly Duke

Dedicated to the survivors—
Debbie, Fayrene, Pat, Laura, Dan,
Kalin, Norman, Margaret,
Chris, and Jodi

ACKNOWLEDGMENTS

Special thanks to the information center at Royal Tunbridge Wells for the wealth of information they provided; to M. Barton for *Tunbridge Wells*; to Roger Fulford for *The Trial of Queen Caroline*; to J. B. Priestley for *The Prince of Pleasure*; to Christopher Hibbert for *George IV: Regent and King*; to Nigel Nicholson and the National Trust for *Great Houses of Britain*; to Sibylla Jane Flower for Debrett's *The Stately Homes of Britain*; to Adrian Tinniswood for *Country Houses from the Air*; to Mary Lyndon Shanley for *Feminism, Marriage and the Law in Victorian England*; to Jeanne P. Deschner for *How to End the Hitting Habit*.

Chapter One

Her laughter won his attention, but it was divorce first brought them together—the Pain and Penalties proceedings—the king's attempt to dissolve his marriage to his all too licentious queen. The brass-founders and coppersmiths of London would do glittering and noisy homage to their beleaguered Queen Caroline. Right down the busiest of thoroughfares to the royal residence they marched on this unseasonably warm fall afternoon, blocking traffic, right and left. Thousands swarmed Piccadilly to view the spectacle.

Two in particular were caught up in the press. Their carriages, headed in opposite directions, slowed to a standstill, side by side. And Melody Bainbridge was laughing, in the face of hardship, in the face of fear, in the face of a nation that made spectacle of itself and its opinions over the proposed separation of its king and queen. Her laughter won Lord Hay's attention away from the inconvenient delay and the distant blare of a brass band.

Laughter was not a sound Lord Hay immediately found engaging or positive. He was not, himself, given to frequent or extended bouts of hilarity. A serious, observant child, he had grown into a serious, observant adult, and as such, too often had he heard the sound of laughter turned against him, a noise denoting not so much delight as it did base misunderstanding, sarcasm, or spite. On occasion, especially with women, it made a coy attempt to win his attention.

This laughter, however, was none of these. Refreshing, pleasant, and unfettered, it flew from the downed window of the glossy black carriage that rolled to a halt beside his, birds of mirth given wing. The sound conjured up for Dunstan Hay, seventeenth Earl of Erroll, an image of the woman from whose lips it spilled.

A pretty young woman, to voice such pretty amusement. A woman of intelligence, wit, and sarcasm. A clever female—the most dangerous kind. His mother was clever, as had been Gillian. He knew well the workings of clever minds. Here was the kind of woman he generally avoided.

All deduced from a laugh, the humor with which he found himself in such unexpected harmony, he involuntarily loosed a low chuckle.

"Hush my dear! Someone hears you." A matronly voice, caustic as a crow's, flapped from the carriage window.

Dunstan hushed himself obediently, but mere words neither clipped nor caged the vibrant wings of this flight of feminine mirth.

"Let them hear, cousin. Especially if it be Burke. I would have him hear my laughter." Her voice was musical, as arresting and impertinent as her laugh. "Too long have I stifled my amusement at the ridiculous. Too long have I stilled humor, opinion, and temper. Fear silenced me. No more, Blanche! This parade, this marvelously ludicrous parade—like the goose who laid golden eggs led before the princess who never laughed—was meant to bring me amusement today."

For a moment he could hear neither what she said, nor what her companion, Blanche, answered. He leaned forward in his seat, curiosity aroused—even went so far as to release the spring, further lowering the window. A sultry breeze wafted into the carriage, the last gasp of summer, and on its breath the odors of the city. London always smelled foul to Dunstan, who far preferred the mild, green, heathery scent of home. This flat, riverside city smelled of too many un-washed humans packed into too few square miles, of too many horses and their offal, of wet pavement and burning coal, of food, ale, obnoxious perfumes used to mask the smells, and always, an undercurrent of the raw reek of sewage in the Thames. It was, com-bined, a smell he associated with his mother. It was always at this time of year he visited her.

"Yesterday it was crystal workers to lift me from the mopes." Like a Highland brook the stranger sounded, clear water chuckling over a rocky bottom. "A glittering cavalcade. Crystal enough that Caroline might have a smashing of it if she so desired. Today, it is coppersmiths and brassfounders, all got up like knights in shining armor. Who will it be tomorrow I wonder?"

"Och, who indeed?" Dunstan murmured. He wanted to laugh with her, to ask her if she had been so fortu-nate as to witness the recent parade of Quakers, for they, too, dour-faced and sober, had taken to the streets in support of the queen, though she was accused of li-centious, offensive, disgraceful, and adulterous behav-ior. Surely such irony was worth a chuckle—but Dunstan, shy of women, especially pert, clever, articu-late young women, was far too polite to intrude upon two to whom he had yet to receive introduction, even with his laughter.

Mounted on white horses, wearing white plumes in their helmets, eight red-faced knights approached, rattling and clanking. Surrounded by brass-hatted squires, these artisans and craftsmen would be knights for a day. Huffing and puffing, they sweated beneath the weight of their conviction and the un-wieldy poundage of too much metal. Brass pikes bris-tled formidably from every fist. Brass helms overhung every brow.

The crowd met them with huzzahs and cheers.

"They look a bit like gladiators! Or is it centurions I mean?" The one called Blanche shouted above the noise.

Roundheads, Dunston thought. They were Roundheads off to storm the castle—an amusing bunch of Roundheads. No blood would be shed.

His dulcet-voiced mystery madame was less charitable. "Little boys playing make-believe in upside-down cook pots, the better for baking already addled brains."

"The hats do look warm," Blanche agreed. "That tall fellow there has taken on a most alarming lobster hue."

Laughter again. Her laughter overpowered all other sounds as far as Dunstan was concerned. Breathless peals of gaiety, an engaging carillon, despite her mean-spiritedness toward his sex, quite contagious under the circumstances because he agreed with her. These men made themselves ridiculous, inviting laughter with a banner that read, "The Queen's Guard are men of metal." Dunstan hastily disguised as an unconvincing cough his involuntary guffaw.

"Melody! Do calm yourself!" Blanche said. "Such a surfeit of uncontrolled laughter is quite uncalled for."

So, his mystery was named Melody, and a complex little tune she was. He would like to see as well as hear this Melody, if only to mark her as a woman to avoid. Such a female would undoubtedly make sport of him as cleverly as she did a troupe of tinsmith knights. The mannerless young ladies in London made habit of finding something laughable in his Scottish accent, in the simple country style of his clothing, in the faux pas he invariably committed when forced to enter into a society far grander than that to which he was accustomed. Certainly he heard stifled giggles and snide remarks whenever he dared to don the family tartan this far south of Aberdeen.

Dunstan leaned out of the window, to no avail. All he could see was the bony backside of the ladies' coachman, who perched on a bullion-trimmed hammercloth of hunter's green. The wheel of the chaise as well. The boxy coachlights. The black leather hood. Frustrated, but struck by an idea, he withdrew into the coach, closed the glass window, shutting out the noise of the crowd, and tapped on the trap above his head.

It opened, admitting the blare of brass, the shouts and laughter, the cheers and applause.

"Aye, milaird?" Swan called.

"Would you be so good as to have the horses take a wee step forward?" Dunstan asked.

"A step, sir? Just the one?"

"Aye. Can you contrive such a thing?"

"Do my best, milaird."

As the trap snapped shut, Dunstan returned to the window and stealthily lowered the glass. His ears were met by a medley of noise. He cocked his head, sifting sound for the one voice that concerned him.

". . . too rich a comedy not to find the fun in it," his Melody was saying. "Laughter, you see, is the language of optimism. I am, ever, the optimist—even now, when I feel as if my every word is overheard, my every move observed."

He wondered what she meant by that. Her voice caught a little in the saying of it. His own breath caught as, jerked briefly into motion, his view changed, the tandem chaise's window sliding by—an impression of fair hair, a bonnet with a feather, a crested door, and then, the horses gone too far, he confronted not the front wheel but the back, with little more to see than the blank black leather of the hindmost part of the coach.

Dunstan sighed, raked a hand through his hair, and looked up, muttering as Swan opened the trap to call, "Does that suit you, milaird?"

"Not quite the desired effect, laddie."

"Beggin' your pardon sir. Canna' hear above yon racket."

"Well enough, man." Dunstan waved him away.

She was laughing again. He longed to observe her, to see if the merriness of a Melody's countenance echoed the merriness of her voice. Dunstan relied heavily on his observations in judging his fellow man—and woman. Faces were maps he had long ago decided. One might see a great deal of the roads a person had chosen by way of their expression.

Was laughter the language of optimism as this Melody would have it? He had always considered laughter the covert voice of cruelty. He leaned against the squabs near the window, the better to determine if his mystery madame was truly the optimist, or merely a hard-hearted young woman unaware of her own callousness.

"Do I detect the hint of a smile, cousin?" she teased. "Admit it. You are as entertained as am I."

"This dreadful divorce is not at all to be laughed at." The Blanche she spoke to did not sound in the least bit amused. "It will be a painful disgrace. You should know that better than anyone."

"Oh, but it is laughable." Her voice sang out above the growing blare of trumpets. "The laws governing divorce must be laughed at, or we should all be weeping at their unfairness. Are you not amused that a king who publicly entertains himself with dozens of paramours would divorce his queen when she but follows his example?"

"But that the queen should exercise such indiscretion as to conduct her affair in a tent, on board a ship with this Bergami fellow! How could she imagine such conduct would remain private?" Blanche asked.

"Better ask how has the king the gall to proclaim his queen in violation of their marriage vows because she conducts an illicit liaison with one Italian nobody when he has bedded, according to rumor, in addition to Mrs. Fitzherbert, Lady Jersey and Lady Conyngham, the daughters of a turnpike keeper, a French courtesan, a Weymouth boardinghouse keeper, and that woman, Mrs. Crow, by whom he is said to have borne a son! It is ludicrous."

She laughed again, the sound flowing over him like water.

Dunstan could not stop a smile from taking possession of his lips. Not optimism, this. Nor was it inherently cruel. Her laughter was aimed at the irony of life, at the frailties and contradictions of the human condition. With such a target, he must laugh along with her.

"It is a mockery of a marriage," Blanche agreed.

His Melody no longer laughed.

"Many marriages are," he thought he heard her say, and could not agree more. Most of his friends, family, and acquaintances found nothing but discontent in the married state. More reason, he thought, never to engage in the tawdry business of one.

"Scandalous in the extreme, this royal inconstancy," Blanche said.

"Scandalous?" Miss Melody had to shout to be heard above the noise of the approaching band. " 'Tis hypocrisy."

Dunstan nodded. Hypocrisy of the highest order!

The band, engulfing all other sound, came lee with the carriages, passed them by, then faded, along with the cheers and shouts.

"All of this marching and posturing in support of a queen who cuckolds her cuckolding husband!" The dulcet voice had taken on a biting tone. "Our laws should be deemed inconstant, rather than the queen."

Dunstan leaned close to the window, that he might stare at what little was to be seen of the woman whose contempt intrigued him even more than her former cheer. Her gloved hand, pale gray, rested briefly on the lip of the windowsill. He had never before found fascination in so little to be seen of a person.

A fluttering of slender fingers, movement like the wing of a dove taking flight, as she said, "You are so good, cousin, to ask me to accompany you in this excursion to the Wells. It will be a blessing to remove myself from London. Away from the noise, the crowds. Away from the feeling I am followed."

Above him, Swan called to his horses, "Walk on."

"Away from this dreadful marriage," the woman named Blanche said flatly.

The coach lurched into motion. Faintly, Dunstan Hay thought he heard his mysterious, melodious Melody echo, "Yes. Away from this dreadful marriage."

Chapter Two

"**D**unstan! You do not attend."

The dowager widow, Lady Hay, Dunstan's mother, peered at him around the silver replica of the Taj Mahal dividing the length of the table they shared for the dinner she insisted he take with her rather than at his club. Her voice, generally a trifle shrill, was exceptionally so when the two of them sat table together. Lady Hay, a creature impressed by pomp and circumstance, insisted that Dunstan, as head of the household, must sit at the head, while she, as an honorable widow, must sit at the foot. Ordinary conversation, when it was attempted, invariably turned into a shouting match.

"Och! I attend well enough," Dunstan muttered wryly, setting aside his spoon, all appetite lost. "It would be rude in me not to, Mother, and you have taught me well with regard to rudeness in conversation. It was marriage you were speaking of. It is, for nigh on a decade now, your favorite topic."

"What's that?" his mother demanded. She was generally impatient when she could not hear him.

"Marriage." He raised his voice. "An institution I've little inclination for engaging in."

Most of the time, rather than shout, a practice which Dunstan abhorred, he busied his mouth with eating during these shared meals, allowing her to hold forth, uninterrupted, on the topic dearest to her heart— finding him a wife.

Her speeches had become repetitive and predictable. Marriage. Weddings. Children. His inheritance. He must be married, should be married, would be married if it was at all within her power to sway him, could be married even now, and to a young woman of spotless reputation, good family, and the proper connections, if he would only apply himself.

She was relentless. As a result, he had become relentlessly resistant. He would not be pushed or prodded, would not place her desires over his own. She had had her way in everything when he was a child. She had had her way with Gillian. He would have his own way now.

A soft-footed invasion of servants swept in to remove the soup bowls, to bring in the second course, and with it the tantalizing odor of wine, mushrooms, and shallots. His mother fell silent. She made a practice of halting conversation whenever underlings entered a room. A private woman, she seemed unable to comprehend that their shouted conversations might be clearly heard, even through closed doors.

"You must think of the continuation of the family name," she grumbled loudly, her color high as she stabbed at the contents of her plate.

Dunstan acknowledged the remark with no more than a nod. The fish, while tastefully presented, looked cold. His mother's kitchen was too distant from the dining room. Food rarely arrived at more than tepid temperatures. He picked at it with his fork—definitely cold. No steam rose from the flaky white flesh.

"You must think of the future, must do your duty, must not dishonor your father, must listen to your mother. I would see you wed before I die. I would dandle a grandchild on my knee—a boy—for a girl will be as good as nothing in keeping the family's fortune intact. And that is of the utmost importance. Surely, you must realize. Surely, you comprehend."

Poached carp. He did not care for carp. Or carping. Never had. He pushed away the dish. Biannually they conducted this largely one-sided discussion, which she considered supremely important and he judged supremely impertinent. Biannually he disappointed her, for more than a dozen years now—once every autumn when he made a point of visiting her London abode in honor of her birthday, and once every summer when she made brief sojourn to the Highlands to escape London's odoriferous heat. He was two and thirty. Too old for lectures. Too old for a mother who believed she might bully him into something he did not care to do. And he did not care to be married— not since Gillian. He was quite content to continue his life as a bachelor, with no one but his valet to order and organize his life. No one to tell him what he must do with himself or his time. No one to smother him, as his mother had as a lad, as a youth, as a young man in love.

Lord Hay loved his only remaining parent, and yet he had never been happier than on the day he left her care. His long, arduous, annual trips sometimes by choppy seas, sometimes over muddy, nigh impassable roads, he considered no more than her due. He must honor the woman if not obey her in all things. He came faithfully to dinner every night he spent in London, and daily sat through the now familiar tirade, unmoved, except to feel a little sad for her, that she wasted so much time and spirit in fruitless persuasion. He allowed himself a modicum of amusement, too, in this argument that quietly raged between them, a stalemate of immovable opposition. It never varied.

That she chose to discuss marriage with him now, when the king and his queen made such a public mockery of theirs, amused him more than usual. The carp stared at him balefully, daring him to allow his smile to dissolve itself in laughter.

His mystery, Melody, would have seen the humor in his mother's viewpoint, in the very manner in which the two of them took dinner together. He imagined her gentle laughter filling the room, and as if, even at a distance, her amusement were contagious, he chuckled out loud over the disapproving head of the untasted fish, the noise ringing in an unexpected moment of stillness as his mother paused to take a breath.

"You laugh?" the dowager, Lady Hay, demanded, her eyes popping in surprise, her second chin waggling furiously, as it had a tendency to do when she was unnerved. "The progression of our name is not a laughing matter!"

Dunstan stilled his laughter and shrugged. "No need to bother yourself about the family name," he called to her. "Barnard and Gillian have eight bairn, five of them lads. He and his offspring happily carry on the family name."

"And happily take over the family fortune, the family estates, the family silver, and all of the china I have collected when you are gone!" She tossed her fork into a plate of the very china to which she referred. "You give me the headache, Dunstan; you do, with this provoking mention of your cousin, Barnard, and his brats."

It was not mention of Barnard that bothered her so much as the one she did not name—Gillian. He had been needlessly cruel, perhaps, in referring to her.

He shoved back his chair and went to pat her awkwardly on the shoulder. "Dinna' fret yourself, Mother." He still found their conversation sadly amusing. "Barnard shall not have any of it until I am pushing up the daisies, and I've no intention of dying young."

She peered up at him, her eyes, like the fish's, baleful, red-rimmed, floating with moisture. More wrinkles troubled their boundaries than he remembered. "You have no intention of marrying then? No desire at all for children? Has there been no one to take your fancy since that dreadful girl . . ." Her voice quavered a bit in asking; she could not voice the name even now—Gillian.

He knelt beside her chair and took her hand in his, patting the blue-veined back of it. Her hand, knuckles knobbier than when last he had held it, reminded him as no clock could, that time passed for both of them.

"Marriage requires a partner one would willingly bind oneself to for the rest o' one's days. I can think of no such female o' my acquaintance."

"You make no great effort to put yourself in the company of eligible females," she spat at him. "Not since . . . not since Barnard's wedding. Are you . . ." Her chin trembled. She bit her lower lip to still it. A tear welled from the corner of her eye. "Are you no longer interested in them?"

"Not particularly," he said truthfully.

"Good God." She blinked furiously, more tears cascading. "Do not tell me . . ."

She covered her mouth with her napkin, unwilling to go on.

"Dinna' tell you what?"

"Do not tell me you prefer . . ."

Again the napkin stifled her.

"What's troubling you? Out with it!"

"Men?" she said.

"Men?" he repeated blankly. Then with a clearer understanding, "You're of a mind I'd be inclined to prefer men?" So unbalanced did the question leave him that he tottered from his knee onto his buttocks.

In an awkward heap on the floor the butler and footmen thus found him as they padded quietly into the room once more to clear away plates and bring in the third course. His view of their neatly shod feet, stepping around and over him, his perspective of their faces as they pretended there was nothing at all unusual in skirting the master lolling about on the floor, made him laugh.

Would that Melody might have been there to laugh along with him.

Uneven splotches of color in his mother's complexion and traces of tears she hastened to wipe from her cheeks sobered him. Stifling his amusement, he rose, breaking the rule of silence in front of the underlings, leaning in over her chair to say mildly, "Nay. I do assure you, Mother. You may be easy. My tastes do not lie in that direction."

"Well, if not for fish, then perhaps you will take a slice of beef," she suggested tartly.

He smiled. She deceived no one but herself in believing every word of their conversation had not been overheard.

"The roast does look more to my liking," he agreed. "As much as English lairds are favored over Scotsmen by the London lasses."

She blinked, sniffed, and waved him away, saying, "Do not hover, Dunstan. You ruin my appetite."

Dunstan was not to be sent back to the far end of the table. "If you will, Jameson, be so good as to reset my place, here." He indicated with the inclination of his head the seat to the right of his mother's.

When Lady Hay opened her mouth to object, he quieted her, saying, "We have much to discuss, and I tire of shouting. I mean to leave London on the morrow."

"Back to Scotland, so soon?"

"Nay. It is not home I'm headed, not yet."

"Where then?"

"To Sevenoaks, in Kent. The Duchess of Dorset has invited me to have a browse in her library."

"The Duchess of Dorset?" She sniffed and seemed to brighten a little. "She has two daughters, has she not?"

"Aye, that she does, and she has promised me something she thinks will take root in Scotland if I do but come and fetch it."

Chapter Three

L ondon left behind him, the fresh, crisp air and the open road revived Dunstan, raised both his spirits and memories of home. All Hallows' Eve he spent at an inn, where a party of young people reveled into the wee hours, bobbing for apples that they might divine their future fortunes, roasting chestnuts that they might foretell their future happiness with a mate. He was invited to join them, but refused with a polite bow. He had no faith in the size of an apple measuring his fortune, nor the burning of a nut to determine his success in marriage. He knew himself for a wealthy man and single, with no intention of changing either state in the near future.

The following day hatched a brilliant robin's egg sky. It seemed a Highland sky as his coach set off again, the perfect cerulean backdrop for the colors of change: russet, amber, burgundy, and brown. The horses seemed restive, drunk on the winelike properties of a freshening breeze, stirred to a brisk trot by the playful chase of leaves that raced and skipped along the road. They made excellent time, reaching Tunbridge Wells at the noon hour, entering the town to the tune of church bells.

Dunstan called a halt to their progress, pausing not to honor saints on this day of saints, but because the weather allowed, because it was on his way to the Duchess of Dorset's estate, and because his mother suffered an arthritic complaint. It troubled her more every winter. The waters of Tunbridge Wells were supposed to do wonders.

He stopped in at Elliot's lending library on his way to the well, that he might sign the register there in order to be included in invitations to any of the local events. He scanned the names above his as he wrote, on the off chance any acquaintance of his should be in the area.

The name Blanche caught his eye, Blanche Claybourne, and while he knew none by that name, the voices of the women watching the brassfounders' parade flooded back to him—the laughter of a Melody. She had mentioned wells to the crow named Blanche. Could it have been Tunbridge Wells, she meant?

The name above Blanche Claybourne's was what looked to say Miss Heverstock, the name below, in clearest cursive, a Lady Bainbridge.

An odd expectation possessed Dunstan, an uneasy anticipation. Was it possible he would see at last the Melody that had eluded him in London? Could she be a Melody Heverstock, or a Melody Bainbridge?

There were two libraries in Tunbridge Wells; one at either end of the tree-lined, fall-touched promenade that led to the Bath House in front of which the town's famed spring was located. Elliot's was at the west end, near the Swan Inn. Beyond the Assembly Rooms, past the olfactory riches of Fishmarket Square, Dunstan located Nash's Library Rooms and Post Office, part of the leaf-strewn square that the Bath House itself formed.

At Nash's, he registered his name again, searching the list as before. No Blanche Claybourne. No Melody, surname unknown. No Miss Heverstock or Lady Bainbridge, either.

Disappointed, he went next to the Bath House where he requested the dipper fill for him a number of cork-topped bottles. She offered to pack them in cotton wool when he indicated he meant to ship them to London. He settled himself then, against one of the stone bases for the slender white columns gracing the window-fronted building, that he might observe the steady parade of elderly and infirm, who would quack themselves with the Spring's waters.

Tunbridge Wells was not the sort of place to interest Dunstan under ordinary circumstances. Peopled by men and women in the impending winter of their lives, their primary topics of conversation centered on the weather, the latest of a variety of aches and pains, and the state of their bowels. The town and its gossip was not at all to his taste.

This week's scandal was Lady Bainbridge, the same Lady Bainbridge from Elliot's directory! Her name was on everybody's lips. Recently descended on the town from London, she was a young woman, he learned, of good family—rumored to be a beauty. But, who could say? She went everywhere, it was said, shrouded in veils. And why? Most thought it no more than an attempt to gain attention, an allurement devised to add mystery to bad manners. Others were convinced the woman was a Queenite, veiling herself in tribute to her beleaguered queen. Caroline was not to be seen in public, according to the papers, without a huge hat and two veils.

"What does it matter her looks?" a pale slip of a woman whispered spitefully.

"Yes. Pretty is as pretty does." The portly gent who said so leaned heavily on his ivory-headed cane, quenched his thirst with six full glasses pumped from the spring, and left the square in a hobbling, water-logged, gout-impeded hurry.

Lady Bainbridge's behavior was deemed the ugliest possible by all who voiced an opinion. She—and Dunstan began to hope with all his heart her first name was not Melody—brought shame to herself and all of those unfortunate enough to be connected to her, by way of her impending—the final word was generally uttered in no more than a whisper—di-vorce.

A woman with an ear trumpet proved an exception

to this rule. In the too loud voice of the deaf she cried out, "Did you say she seeks a separation?"

"-shun, -shun." Her shocked voice echoed from the stone face of the Bath House along the shady, colonnaded walkway, turning heads and stilling tongues.

"From her spouse of four years," a humpbacked woman shouted into her hearing device.

"-ears, -ears," bounced ironically from the triangular pit in which the spring was housed.

"Just like the king and queen!" a red-faced young man with a complexion complaint roared into the horn.

With a hound dog shake of her lace-lappeted head the old woman complained, "No need to shout."

"Out! Out!" her echo insisted.

Dunstan laughed, and as he did he listened. Had his easily amused Melody been anywhere in Bath Square, he was sure she would have found the gossip with regard to poor Lady Bainbridge as diverting as did he. But of his mystery he heard nothing. He laughed alone.

The dipper at last finished with the task of bottling and crating his mother's water, he prepared to leave the well, to continue his progress to the Duchess of Dorset's.

The approach of two women along the flagstoned walkway stopped him. A spate of gasps and whisperings accompanied their appearance.

"There *she* is."

"Hush. She comes."

"Only see how brazen she looks in that silly veil."

Dunstan looked, as did everyone. There was a veil. Like a dying leaf it trembled in the wind. She was clad in the colors of the season, all buff and brown velvet, claret-colored ribbons and amber merino, as if the leaves that whirled about her skirts had taken delightful human form. Alluring, yes. Nothing brazen about her. Quite to the contrary. Lady Bainbridge looked every inch the lady.

Here was the sort of female who substantiated his

reluctance to wed, a woman who went to the enormous trouble and expense required to separate herself from a husband she had sworn to love, honor, and obey till death did they part. A woman fickle of feeling, a woman without tenacity enough to stick to her vows of love, of obedience, of forever after. Here was not his Melody. He read no trace of laughter, of humor, in this stiff-backed female, only a guarded intrigue, a hint of the tainted and knowing, the forbidden and provocative. Dunstan longed to lift the veil, to face the enemy, as it were, eye to eye.

Chapter Four

She grew weary of hiding the truth, of denying the past, of peering through a net-blurred haze at her narrowed view of the world. And yet she valued the face-framing leghorn. It could not stop people from peering, but the veiled hat did stop them from seeing.

A popular place for peering, Bath Square. The largely octogenarian set who came to sip the mineral waters stood about in front of the Bath House, cups teetering in palsied, arthritic, blue-veined hands, sharing the latest news before they downed their daily dosage of chalybeate bitters. One might so pause only before the water was swallowed, Blanche had informed her. It would not do to pause once the liquid was taken, lest one's bowels betray one in public.

The prospect of purgative waters left Melody undaunted. She was ready to be cleansed of all that was waste in her life, all that filled her with regret, with pained memory, with fear. Arm in arm, bolstering one another, she and Blanche made their way along the Parade, their approach, like the tossing of a stone into a pond, sending ripples of silence before them. Mouths pursed as they approached, whispers hushed. A few in the gauntlet of aged and infirm threw them sidelong glances. Most deliberately turned their backs or hid behind unfurled parasols and fans. No one wished them good day. No one nodded or smiled.

In the uneasy quiet a voice exploded. "Is she the one?"

A sour-faced matron with an earhorn glared at

them as they passed. When whisperers at either elbow would hush her, she spoke even louder, her voice harsh, "I do not care if she does hear! It is not fitting. Not permitted when I was a young woman! Leaving one's husband! Creating such a stir."

Another woman, a fishwife from the nearby market if the stains on her apron were to be trusted, nodded vigorously, chins waggling. "What ill does she hope to mend with our waters, I wonder? They will heal neither broken vows nor a broken maidenhead!"

Her crass remark provoked uneasy bleats of laughter. It stopped Blanche in her tracks. But without the slightest indication she heard either woman, Melody sailed past them, head high.

She was pleased her step never faltered—not so pleased to find herself keenly observed by a gentleman, perched like an observant kestrel at the base of three of the slender columns that edged the dipper's domain. The dipper, a round-eyed girl, also stood staring.

The almost expressionless bird was not handsome so much as he was noble in appearance. A local tradesman or landowner, perhaps, dressed simply as was the country style—even the colors and patterns of his plumage resembling those of a falcon. His was a chestnut brown coat, high-collared, a buff and brown-spotted waistcoat, doeskin breeches, and cuffed brown boots. Light, almost airy brown hair was swept back from a high forehead under an old-fashioned, wide-brimmed black hat with a leather band that buckled above his brow.

His nose overshadowed a mouth tight set and a chin of chiseled strength. His eyes were green, birdlike only in their keenness. He scanned her, head to toe. He was a man, and as such, felt free to stare at her. For that alone, she decided, he was worthy of contempt.

She did not shrink before his implacable, green-eyed regard. It reminded her too much of Burke. By such fixed looks he had once intimidated her.

No longer. Never again.

Chin set, spine straight, she shut out the whispering, the sly looks, the stomach-churning fear of a past to which she need never return. As if she might prove herself to all men in facing down this stranger's attempted intimidation, she squared her resolve along with her shoulders and stepped past him to reach with steady hand for the dipper's offering.

The cup was full, the attendant clumsy. Water sloshed, soaking her glove.

"Careless girl," Blanche snapped, shaking her water-stained skirt.

Melody sighed. Spills were no great thing, certainly unworthy of ill-tempered scolding.

"Never mind, my dear," she said. "Amid life's troubles what is one wet glove?" Her words were perfect. She was ever careful of them. Words possessed power. Burke had taught her that much. Both Blanche and the apologetic dipper believed her carefully chosen words meant for them. Both women smiled, appeased. In squelching what might have proved a volatile exchange, Melody took immeasurable relief. She laughed.

Her laughter, familiar and welcome, closed his eyes. Like the gentle pulse of water from the well, it washed over him, as sweet as her voice in speaking so kindly to the mortified dipper. Here was his Melody after all! Here his laughing maiden, still faceless, though he now had figure and form with which to identify her, and a name, Lady Bainbridge, of shocking reputation.

Briskly stripping sodden kid from her hand, Melody Bainbridge accepted the linen towel the attendant was quick to hand her and pressed the drenched glove between its folds.

He watched her every movement with renewed interest, watched the supple bend and sway of her, the waft of her veil as she moved, the nimble dexterity of her fingers, never still, as she went about her task. He would have sworn she wore a bracelet—a band of odd, misshapen plum-colored stones—his mind would accept no other explanation until she slid fingers into damp leather and smoothed buff kid over palm and wrist, no bulge to mar the line of her extremities.

Melody smoothed away all wrinkles, smoothed away bad memories, hiding once again her shame, evening out the color with which she met the world beneath a thin shield of damp kid. Head high, she turned to hand the soggy linen to the apologetic attendant.

"Here you are, my dear." Blanche held out the cup she had forgotten.

Melody considered the liquid with consternation. Perhaps it was not such a good idea after all, coming to the Wells. She had hoped to remove herself from the public eye, from a whirl of gossip, from prying questions. And yet, she was unable to so much as swallow a glass of water without exposing herself.

The multipaned windows of the Bath House regarded her as searchingly as the square full of gossips at her back. There was only the pure white trio of columns she might face without fear of being observed by a great mob, and that direction was occupied as well. One falcon, however, seemed lesser evil than a flock of cackling carrion feeders.

Defiantly, therefore, Melody faced the gentleman who stared at her, lifted her veil, bunching it high enough that she might drink, and downed the flat, faintly metallic contents of the cup in a single gulp.

Anger flooding her along with the water, she paused before lowering the veil into place again, to look the gentleman straight in the eye.

The fierce challenge of her gaze shamed him. He ought not stare, and yet he could not look away. How strange the fulfillment of his hopes. How tragic the revelation of evil he had longed to expose. Lady Bainbridge, his mysterious laughing Melody, was not the tainted, forbidden, knowing enemy he had anticipated. Far from it. She had a pale, almost ethereal visage, fine-boned and delicately proportioned. Her eyes seemed bluer, her skin fairer by contrast to the jaundiced purpling of the bruises she would hide, the same plum color as ran rings around her wrist.

He winced to think how hard the blows had to have fallen. The bow of her mouth as she drank was exaggerated, a little lopsided with swelling. Skin, once broken, was now on the mend.

Here was an evil exposed, well enough, just not the one he had expected.

Too acutely she felt the strength of this stranger's understanding, his expression sober, kind, and unexpectedly sweet. She could not—would not—trust it to be real. She had too readily trusted in the past. She would not be fooled again.

It was the attendant who inhaled abruptly, in danger of spilling more water. He did not gasp, her perched falcon, and yet he had seen. She knew he had. His expression changed little beyond a slight narrowing of his eyes, a faint creasing of his forehead. Melody glanced swiftly from the dipper's horrified expression to the collected compassion in a pair of green eyes, no longer blank of feeling, brim full instead of an empathy so unexpected her hand shook as she set aside the emptied cup. Beneath the cool falcon facade was a man warm enough to be shocked by her bruises.

She turned to go.

A wave of whispering arose from those incapable of compassion.

"Ready?" Blanche asked softly when she faltered.

Melody nodded, chin down, staring at the gauzy view of her feet. Water roiled uncomfortably in her stomach. Dizzy, weak-kneed, every rude stare, disapproving frown, and spiteful whisper sapped her of strength.

With the skid of leather on flagstone, the gentleman beside the fountain abandoned his perch. Boot heels clapped. She started uneasily, jerked back from the waft of stirred air as his hat was swept from his head. For an instant she cowered, though he offered nothing more dangerous than a better view of the soft brown sweep of his hair. How foolish to feel threatened by the obeisance any well-bred gentleman observed in greeting or taking his leave of a lady—a formal bow.

A bow—nothing more, nothing less—a simple gesture. It took no more than a moment. A trifle forward as they had yet to be introduced, and yet so great was her relief, she took no offense. Quite the reverse. With the removal of his hat and a polite bend at the waist, the stranger reminded Melody she was a lady, and as such, worthy of respect.

Donning his hat, he murmured as he walked away, his voice softened by an unmistakable burr, "A good day to you, ladies."

A good day. It could prove a good day, yet, if she chose to make it so.

Head high, Melody linked her arm through Blanche's. Together, they turned their backs on the highly touted healing waters of Tunbridge Wells.

Chapter Five

Cradled in the palm of his gardening glove, the sapling and its dirt seemed fragile and pale, too fragile to survive the trip to Scotland, and yet Dunstan had high hopes. This tender shoot of life, given the right soil, light, water, and temperatures, might one day be a cherry tree. It was cherries, after all, brought him to Knole, not the Duchess of Dorset's daughters as his mother might hope, blooms too young to tempt him, and not at all ripe in their thinking.

The sapling, tender and yet not too green, reminded Dunstan of Lady Bainbridge, the woman at the well, his laughing Melody. She had not been given the right soil in which to grow a marriage—not according to the bruises on her face and wrist. He wondered at the potential of such a fragile, misused creature. He hoped she might find the right conditions in which to flourish. His thoughts turned too much in her direction these past few days, a woman whose path he would likely never cross again.

Even as thoughts of her passed through his head, he looked beyond the seedling cherry, toward the house, toward a movement of sight-seers just strolling into view from the boundary of shrubbery that sheltered Knole's bowling green. For an instant, there she was, cupped in his palm, along with the sapling. Melody Bainbridge!

She was enrobed, not in the colors of fall, but in a dark, cherry red velvet pelisse. A froth of pale netting draped tastefully from a deep-brimmed straw bonnet. Her dress was a blossom of white muslin trimmed in pink and sprigged with the same black that blighted the cherry velvet with sleeve caps and lapel facings. Her companion, not the crow he had first envisioned, looked a plump pigeon, in gray and violet.

He could not believe his eyes.

The vision was not his imagination. He could not blink her away. The two women strolled toward the orchard. They would soon reach the neat rows of cherry trees among which he knelt, bagging saplings, and up to his elbows in filth.

Flushed with a heat of anticipation, foolish for flushing, Dunstan stood, and in standing dropped the tree he held. He felt even more foolish in bending to catch it up, minus a few leaves and most of one of its baby branches. Clipping back the damaged bits, he packed the tender root system in one of the waiting bags of peat.

"They'll never survive," he had been warned, but he refused to be less than optimistic. Cherries required a bit of cold in order to fruit. Perhaps these Morellos, protected in a walled garden and nursed through their first few winters, might see fit to live.

He was dampening down the root ball when he caught sight of her again, of her patterned skirt, anyway, when she paused in the pathway before him to say uncertainly, even defensively, her back rigid, "I would thank you, sir, if you will be so good as to tell me to whom I am indebted."

He stood—too abruptly.

She started, fell back a step.

Awkwardly, he removed his hat, dipped his head to don it again; then, disconcerted by the sight of his own muddy gloves clutching the brim, he shucked one of the gloves and doffed the hat again, all the while letting his eyes travel from the hem of her skirt to the peak of her veiled bonnet. Like bruised fruit she stood before him, waiting to be eaten or discarded. Her companion, the Blanche creature, hung back, eyeing him uneasily from the end of the pathway.

"Dunstan Hay," he said gruffly, his voice unused to speaking, so many hours had he spent alone. "At your service, my lady. I dinna' ken. In what way would I be deserving of your appreciation, Lady Bainbridge?"

"I would thank you for your kindness." She said it stiffly, as if she disliked the idea of being obliged to him in any way.

"Kindness?" He was confused. "What kindness?"

"You wished me a good day. None others deemed me worthy."

"Have you come to wish me a good day in return, so that you may no longer feel indebted?" he asked.

She seemed taken aback, as if this was not at all the reply she had expected. Confusion unsettled her voice as she gestured to his row of burlap-bagged trees. "I can see I interrupt your work, sir. I shall trouble you no more."

She turned to go.

"Och! No need to hurry on your way. I am just done here." He was unwilling to let her depart with nothing but brusque words and uneasy manners. This fragile creature had already suffered much at the hands of man. He would not leave her with the impression he intended to add to her distress. Without haste, for he knew sudden movement unsettled her, he stripped the second soil-encrusted glove from his hand and slipped the stained apron from his waist. "Is it a tour o' the house and gardens you are taking?"

"Yes, but we are told the duchess entertains guests. That the poor of the neighborhood will come a-souling today." She spoke too fast. She was nervous he supposed, though the idea that he should unsettle her baffled him. "The housekeeper has her hands full handing out cakes and no time to traipse us about the place. Are you gardener here? I've no wish to detain you if you, too, are busier than usual."

He smiled. She thought him a gardener, did she? "A gardener, o' sorts, I am," he admitted languidly, "but no' here at Knole. I am, like you, a visitor, given gracious leave to take some saplings home with me."

"And is home Scotland? You have the lilt of the Highlands in your voice." Her tone was edgy, uneasy.

"'Tis. I hope these cherries may learn to weather our brawny winters. It is no' a climate or a landscape where the fragile survive." He studied her as he said it, wondering if she could survive the lonely chill of the Highlands—doubting it.

"Melody, my dear, shall we continue our perambulations?" The Blanche approached.

"I could show you about the place, ladies, if you've no objection to a guide." The words blurted from his mouth without forethought, startling Dunstan as much as they would seem to have startled Lady Bainbridge.

"Thank you, but . . ." she did not sound at all inclined to take advantage of his offer, which was just as well, for Dunstan was not at all sure now that he had done so, why he had offered.

"That would be very kind of you." It was the pigeon, the Blanche, who surprised them all, in accepting.

Melody thought Mr. Hay meant to show them about the gardens, and at first he did just that, leading them through the neat rows of plantings that the cooling weather had only peripherally begun to brown, pointing out rare specimens, his voice thick, warm, and sweet as treacle. He identified shrub and flower by name, fondly—as if he spoke of friends.

Some distance from the house, he turned. "My favorite view."

It was a fair prospect, made fairer by the day, so brisk and clear, the sky awash with blue, the distant trees aflame with color. Down the main walkway Melody's gaze was drawn, past rows of potted plants and carefully clipped shrubs, across the bowling green, its emerald hue gone tawny, past a distant fringe of color, a knot garden, to the house itself—huge, gable-roofed in red-brown, walled in golden gray ragstone with boxy, crenellated watchtowers. Triple rows of mullioned windows, like multifaceted eyes, watched her, disapprovingly, perhaps, as she had neither house nor hovel to call her own.

"It looks more Jacobean village than house from this distance," she said weakly, turning her back on the embodiment of all that had been lost to her. "A lovely prospect."

"Aye." He nodded, his gaze fixed on her rather than the house. "Bonnie." His gaze, so green, seemed to see straight through her veil, straight into her very thoughts. Such warmth, the very feeling that Mr. Hay regarded her much as he did the plants he had fondly pointed out to them, unnerved her. She was not certain she wanted to be friends with any man just yet, even a gentlemanly gardener.

Uneasy, she set out along one of the pathways that led obliquely toward Knole. He fell into step beside her, a position she had allowed only Blanche to assume thus far in their stroll. Uncomfortable, she clasped hands together in the small of her back, that her sleeve might not chance to brush his.

He offered up to her not his arm, but a sentence, more words than he had, as yet, strung together. "As many rooms as there are days in the year, Knole is said to have, and fifty-two staircases—in numbers to match the weeks."

"So many?" Blanche fell into step behind them. "How exhausting. And how many servants to climb about those dreadful stairs?"

"Not quite two hundred I am told," he said, his voice soft, his tone such that Melody knew she would find him smiling if she but turned to look at him. She would not turn her head, could not bring herself to face the depths of his green eyes, even from behind the shield of her veil.

"Dear me!" Blanche exclaimed.

"A singing village," Melody declared with a laugh. Indeed there was the faint sound of singing to be heard from the direction of the house.

Mr. Hay was smiling at her, the smile as slow and gentle as his voice, his sober countenance transformed.

"A 'Souling' party," he said, "begging for soul cakes. A pretty custom, to sing for the dead, think you not?"

She nodded curtly, and said no more.

It was Blanche who kept the man busy with questions as they turned and followed the row of trees that marked the edge of the deer park surrounding Knole. Melody found herself run dry of questions, of witty responses, of all enthusiasm, in fact, for this tour of an estate she had long wished to see. Melancholy possessed her.

This grand and beautiful place, the voices raised in song, touched upon the wounded longing in her, the dashed dreams of acting mistress to the manor. It was what she had been born to do, or so her parents had repeatedly informed her. She could not help but think of her parents often today, on this day of remembering the dead. In the responsibilities of managing property and household she had been thoroughly schooled. Of the mending of one's heart, of one's very existence, after one's parents died, after a marriage gone sour, she knew next to nothing.

Nearby, a church bell tolled in honor of the dead. Ahead of them, in the lane that bordered the trees, she spied a roan. The sight of such a horse set her pulse racing. Burke favored roans. She shook herself, shook away the clutch of fear. Burke was in London, not in the wilds of the Kentish countryside. He was certainly not the only man in the British Isles to ride a roan.

"This way. I shall just take you in by way o' the Green Courtyard." Mr. Hay's gentle voice intruded upon her uneasy rumination.

"He means to show us the house?" Melody asked Blanche with some alarm as they quit the gardens and crossed the carriageway, heading for the gatehouse guarding the west front.

Blanche nodded.

"You mean to show us the house, Mr. Hay?" Melody judged her own voice too shrill.

"You've still a yen to see it, have you no'?" Contrary to hers, his voice, his manner, his very mien, were as mild as milk. Meek, gentle—she found his very blandness irritating. Why did she hesitate to trust him? To allow herself to believe any man so genial as this one?

"Will we not be in the way?" She could not tell him she had lost all desire to see the house; it was not entirely true. And yet, she feared he meant to overstep his bounds. Certainly he overstepped hers. "I should not like to intrude, to cause a fuss," she claimed.

"You've no wish to sing a song for a soul cake, then?"

"None at all." The words sounded harsher than she had intended.

His eyes were the only part of his face not entirely mild. There were depths in them unplumbed, a bit of curiosity, of mischief, even sadness. "I have been given free run of the place. I would not presume to go where I am not welcome. Nor would I take you where you've no wish to go. Never fear."

And yet she did fear. For too many years had she lived steeped in fear. It ran rampant in her. She feared her divorce would not be granted, feared the power her husband and the courts still held over her future. She feared she would never be able to call any home her own again, feared her reception by polite society hence forward would be a cool one. She feared the very man before her.

All men, even this gardener, were too charming on the surface, too well spoken, too well educated, too full of promises and good cheer. This gentleman gardener, of whom Blanche seemed too readily to approve, she feared for his very maleness, for his gentle-voiced kindnesses, for his captivating eyes. He seemed bent on ingratiating himself with her, just as Burke had.

Aware of her reluctance, wondering what it was in him displeased her, he led her into Knole by way of the Green Courtyard, pointing out the bit known to the servants as "Shelly's Tower." It had been inhabited briefly by a mistress of the third Duke of Dorset. Her name, Baccelli, had proved too difficult to pronounce.

The beauty of the woman to whom he recounted this history was history herself, an unstable memory, like the face of a house glimpsed through the arch of a gateway. He longed to have it verified again, longed to lift the veil that completely walled in her reactions to his tale until she said, "And what did the duchess think of this mistress Baccelli?"

"I know not," he answered truthfully.

"Then tell me what sort of woman the duchess was."

Dunstan shrugged. "Arabella Diane Cope was her name, a woman o' means and beauty."

"Let me guess," she stopped him sardonically. "She brought her husband fine bloodlines, an excellent reputation, and a great deal of money."

"Aye, all of this, but no happiness. He is said to have grown taciturn and tight-fisted in their years together."

"He was, I daresay, free-wheeling and ready with the cash as a young man?" Lady Bainbridge bit out the words.

Dunstan nodded, wondering, and not for the first time, what manner of man Lord Bainbridge was. What had coaxed this young woman to marry a brutal man?

"He was handsome?" she asked. "Engaging? Did he charm her into believing herself beloved?"

He nodded, wishing he might ask her the same questions, delivering the line in his story with which he had hoped to make her laugh. "He is said to have disguised himself as a gardener to pursue an intrigue with Lady Derby."

"A gardener?"

She did not laugh. He was disappointed.

Blanche allowed a little huffing sound of amusement. "How very appropriate then, that you should reveal to us this story," she said brightly.

He had thought so too, but Lady Bainbridge turned her back on him abruptly, veil flying, gravel grinding beneath her boot. "From your description, Mr. Hay, the duchess had to have been as unhappy in marriage as was the duke."

"Mayhap you are right," he said agreeably, in no mood to further provoke her.

"I am sure of it," she said firmly. "What woman would not despise the man for his many indiscretions?"

"A woman in love," he suggested.

His answer did nothing to calm her. Quite to the contrary. With an explosive sound indicating her displeasure, she flung back the opinion, "A woman in love would have despised him all the more!"

Chapter Six

Who was this man, this impudent gardener, who would seem bent on provoking her? Melody could not deny her curiosity; neither could she deny the grating irritation she felt in conversing with Mr. Hay. Men in general irritated her, had rubbed her the wrong way often since she had separated herself from Burke, in whom she had read no evil, no lies, no potential for violence. She had not seen the truth because she, unlike the long dead Duchess of Dorset, had been blinded by love.

Resentful, then, of his intrusion upon their excursion, upon history she would just as soon forget as face, Melody held her tongue as they were escorted into the house.

It was a staircase, the Grand Staircase, that led her and the quiet, watchful Mr. Hay to a better understanding. Recently renovated, this lovely Jacobean flight of fancy intrigued Melody with its very excess. They came upon it at a moment when the sun poured like a ghostly presence through diamond-paned windows set with heraldic glass. The lower flight was thrown into cool shadow, the upper drenched in a gold that gilded the spotted backs of the leopard newel posts, threw into harsh shadows the grotesque faces that peered at one from the mannerist strapwork, and visually flattened the trompe l'oeil balusters painted along the wall. Ionic columns supported highly embellished arches through which one stepped.

But nothing drew the eyes so much as the figures

worked on every wall. Off-white, creamy yellow, muted fern green and gray, the painted surfaces, like book plates, picturing myth or allegory, were a delight to behold.

"Lovely!" Melody gasped as they ascended the stair. "Unlike anything I have ever seen before."

"You might have done something similar to the old staircase at Bainbridge Hall, given half a chance," Blanche whispered.

Melody frowned, her pleasure dimmed. "No good bemoaning what will never be, Blanche," she said tersely.

"Who would have guessed the old house would be sold the very week of your wedding?"

"Indeed. Who would have guessed a great many things?" Melody, who had no desire to air her dirty linen in front of Mr. Hay, hoped Blanche would hold tongue.

Mr. Hay politely pretended he heard not a single word of their exchange. He did, in fact, lead them into safer conversational territory by pointing out a painting hung in the long, echoing ballroom through which he preceded them.

"Thomas Sackville. He is responsible for the stairway and for most of the renovations that please you. His grandson Richard, on the other hand"—he pointed to another portrait, another soul for the singing—"almost lost the place out of carelessness, high living, and bad habits."

The men in both paintings observed them coolly from on high.

"Habits?" Blanche prodded.

"Aye. The habits of most men who go out of their way to displease their wives: wine, women, gambling, and a great pile of debts, of which he hoped marriage might relieve him."

"He sounds a horrid man," Melody said.

"Not horrid. Nooo. You are too severe. A horrible husband, yes, weak-willed and self-indulgent. Certainly he was a poor manager o' his money, but he was not ill thought of by all."

"One might say the same of the most shameful of souls, think you not?" She said it tartly. "I am sure even Attila the Hun, who had his brother killed before pillaging half a dozen nations, was not ill-thought of by someone. Perhaps his mother found some little thing in him to love."

"Aye." He laughed. "Most probably his mother and perhaps the sister of the Emperor Valentinian as well. She did, after all, offer to marry him."

Melody was not pleased with his flippant attitude, too put out to wonder why a gardener would speak with any knowledge of ancient emperors. "I think The Scourge of God's wife loved peace more than she regarded her spouse," she snapped. "In marrying him she saved her father's lands and the people dwelling therein from certain plunder."

"Och, well, many a poor marriage in the British Isles has been thus arranged." He said it with a one-eyed squint that came very close to approximating a wink. "It was not so very different an arrangement for Richard here. Would you not agree?"

She would not agree, and she would not tolerate his winking at her, but before she could tell him as much, Blanche said, "He does not look the complete rascal."

"Rascals seldom do." Temper rising, Melody fixed her gaze on Mr. Hay. *He* did not look the rascal as he stood staring at a full-length portrait of a sweet-faced young woman wearing paniers, a high ruched collar, and fan-shaped cuffs. Sun limned his profile, struck hints of gold in his hair. But all men were rascals at heart, were they not?

"Here you see Anne Clifford, wealthy daughter of a wealthy buccaneer." He turned. "She was perceived as Richard's financial salvation, the poor dear. But he got more than he bargained for in marrying her."

"Did he now?" she asked wryly, primed for verbal badinage.

"Aye. She was a canny one." He said it as if he had

known the woman personally, as if, in fact, he held her in very high regard. "Would not give him her money to squander as he had his own. Quite clever when it came to keeping accounts, the Lady Anne."

"Her inheritance was willed to her specifically, then?" Melody found herself much interested in financial affairs of late, her own having been left in such a dreadful state.

"Aye, and as such, became the source o' a number of lawsuits."

"A wise father to have so arranged the thing," Blanche said.

Melody simmered, nothing to add. Her own father had not proven so wise.

"I understand she gave him back his ring at one point," Mr. Hay said quietly. Again he looked her way, and she was struck by the thought, as she had been the first time she had felt his stare, that he seemed to see right through her veil, into the very heart of her. Disconcerting, he was.

"Gave him back his ring, did she?" Clinging for a moment to her own empty ring finger, Melody focused all attention on the face in the painting. She began to like this Lady Anne more and more.

"Aye, and he stole their daughter from her at another." He continued to watch her, as if he could read her feelings by way of movement or gesture. The intensity of his attention was bothersome.

The blow, when it came, blindsided her, for it was Blanche who knocked her unsteady in saying, "Thank God you had not children to contend with."

The remark was so unexpected, so uncalled for, so wounding, Melody was struck speechless.

"She has a melancholy look about her," Mr. Hay said gently.

Melody recovered her tongue. "She had little to cheer her with such a greedy wastrel for a husband."

Unfazed by her acid tone, he agreed. "Too true. He left her much o' the time to her own devices. Bowling and tilting he was fond of, and watching the local cockfights and horse races. He adored high stakes, fine clothes, expensive females, and fighting o'er his wife's land and money. Ann found little happiness as his wife."

Melody wanted to hold onto her anger. The burning drive of it made her feel alive, as if she could change things, as if it revenged the ways in which she had been wronged, but her past was history, as unchangeable as that of the woman in the portrait. Anger was a pointless waste of energy when the man before her did and said nothing deliberately offensive. Her gaze traveled the length of the finely accoutred room. "Poor lady." The spark of her ire waned, leaving her spent and out of sorts. "I wonder what she did to keep up her spirits?"

Mr. Hay was ready with an answer. "Played cards with the steward, baked rosemary cakes, embroidered pillows, and allowed the French page to convince her that all o' the male servants in the house loved her."

She had not expected an answer, certainly did not expect him to continue, saying, "At night when she must have been loneliest—"

"Sir!" She interrupted him.

"Perhaps you had better not tell us." Even Blanche sounded sharp.

Mr. Hay ducked his head, his face coloring. "'Tis naught improper, ladies, what I would tell you."

"No?" Melody's tone was cold, her cheeks hot.

His brows arched in unison. "Nay," he said defensively.

Blanche diffused the building tension between them in asking, "How do you know so many intimate details in the life of this Lady Anne?"

"I have been reading her diaries," he admitted openly, as if it were not at all unusual for a gardener to be reading a lady's private papers. "They are part o' the Sackville library, of which I have been given permission to browse as I will. It was Lady Anne who was greatly responsible for the planting of some of the rarities in the gardens."

Melody had not expected him to be a reader, this dirt-digging Scotsman. That he read a woman's diary, the better to understand the house and gardens in which he was a guest, impressed her despite her every inclination to the contrary.

"What did she do then, at night?" She was blushing. She could feel the heat in her neck, in her face. It throbbed in the bruises beside eye and mouth. Thank God he had no view of her complexion. Her voice sounded cool enough.

"Lady Anne was a great reader. Her secretary was given the task o' copying bits of her favorite texts and maxims, which she pinned inside the curtains o' her bed."

"So, she read her bed curtains when she had trouble sleeping?" Melody eyed the portrait with even greater empathy. "No doubt she read alone."

"So goes the tale."

"Poor lamb," Blanche cooed.

"Not my idea of an ideal marriage." Anger rose again in Melody, tempting her.

"Nay, nor mine," he agreed. "I mean to light a candle for her this evening."

Disarmed, and yet wary of such softness in a man, of the kindly glow in his eyes as he gazed at the portrait, of his allowing that same kindness to shine on her when he looked her way, Melody asked brusquely, expecting the worst, "How did it end for her?"

He tilted his head, squinted at the ceiling, and raised his eyebrows for a moment with an expression she could only describe as chagrin. "Sackville died. She married again. A triumph of optimism, don't you know."

"And did this triumph of optimism bring her happiness?" she asked skeptically.

He smiled, ducked his head, and shook it. "I regret to tell you it did not."

"Her triumph a failure then," she suggested, not at all surprised, seeking, in fact, confirmation of her growing belief that wedded bliss was no more real than the grisaille gods and goddesses depicted in Knole's Grand Staircase.

"Nay," he protested. "Failure is surely too harsh a word. I know little more than that they were a quarrelsome couple and she outlived him. She went home then and found true purpose in restoring her castles in Westmorland and in entertaining her many grandchildren. She lived to the ripe auld age of eighty-six."

"A happy ending, after all," Blanche said brightly.

"If not happy, may we, each of us, find such contentment," Hay agreed. The lilt of his accent lent the words a lyrical note.

Melody turned away abruptly, moved by Lady Anne's story, equally moved by Mr. Hay's sentiments in revealing that story to them.

They stepped into another of several galleries, Dunstan following close upon Melody's heels, concerned the telling of Lady Anne's story had been unwise.

"Does it bother you to hear of Lady Anne and her—"

"Failed marriages?" she suggested sharply.

The violence of her reaction backed him up a step. Recovering, aware she had good reason to voice occasionally her anger, he fell in beside her to say, "Unhappy marriages I'll grant you, but Lady Anne seems no failure to me. She did as she saw fit, the best she could do given her options."

"I take it you have heard of my failed marriage?" Her words were crisp, brittle, sardonic.

"I have heard you left your husband." Concern crept into his voice. "That you hope to be granted a divorce."

"I have and I do," she agreed coolly, walking away, as if to distance herself from the subject.

"And was it the best you could do, given your options?" he asked.

She whirled to face him. "How dare you ask!"

"You're not forgettin' I have seen what you hide beneath that pretty veil o' yours? It was he bruised your face, was it no'?"

"It is none of your business." The words emerged high-pitched and shaken, as if a little girl took possession of her vocal cords.

"True enough." His accent thickened, along with the tension in his voice. "But if it were, I would no' hesitate to tell you, no point in hangin' about for more of that, now, is there?"

She shrugged. "The rest of society would not agree with you."

"The rest o' society?" He chuckled. "Whoever that may be, may never have suffered having their face pummeled for no good reason."

She laughed. Ah, how he loved the sound of it.

"Would that the judges agree with you."

"They will."

"You sound confident."

She sounded sarcastic.

"Surely, the judges are men o' good sense."

She laughed again. "I am not so sure. It is men, after all, who have passed into law the ruling that all that was mine is now my husband's because I would not stay under his thumb, depending upon his care, his roof, and his uneven temper while these same sensible judges take their time determining whether I am to be legally separated from a man to whom I will never, willingly, return."

"Glad I am to hear of it, and I am certain all will work out well for you, my lady."

"I should very much like to distill your confidence. I would pour it, if I could, like fine wine, into a tightly corked bottle, and now and again, when my spirits ebb and I wonder why men alone are given the power to decide my fate, I would swallow a mouthful, for I am in dire need of confidence and optimism."

"But you are an optimist," he said with quiet certainty.

"Why should you suppose such a thing?"

"Why?" He tried to see beyond the veil, to understand why she would question her own hopefulness. "Because you had the courage to hope for a brighter future. Surely, that is prime evidence. As is your laughter. Is it no' the language of optimism?"

Galleries leading into galleries, he directed them onward, and, outside again, courtyards into court-yards—the large and formal, leading to the informal, which led farther, to the very intimate closed off spaces that few saw. Private inner spaces, guarded on all sides from view, from the world. These were the inner recesses of Knole, and in them Dunstan saw a strong resemblance between the old house and the young woman whose veil shut him out almost com-pletely.

Of all the rooms they viewed, the Cartoon Gallery was most like Melody Bainbridge. Long and dark, a wall of shuttered windows had to be thrown open to the light, the better to see the richly hued display of a number of enormous painted studies that had once served as models for tapestry design—the Raphael cartoons. A beautiful room, the ceiling plastered and dadoed in an unusual serpentine pattern, it boasted an attractive floor-to-ceiling marble fireplace, the po-tential heat of which faced exquisite Raphaelesque pilasters framing each of the inset windows. Lavish intaglio was picked out on walls and window casings in a tasteful color scheme, richly gilded, an abundance of caryatid figures, raised birds, monkeys, and gar-lands of fruit. The Sackville ram's head crest guarded every inset window shutter.

All was complex pattern, rich color, light and shadow, all except the floor made of massive, rough-hewn golden oak planking. The tight-fitted wood a great deal uneven in its placement, drew the eye as much, perhaps more than any of the room's polished fineries. The planks staggered drunkenly one way and then the other, gross imperfection in a room of in-numerable perfections.

"How wonderful!" she said.

"Aye. Fond o' the flooring, I am," he admitted. "Oak trees, you see, split right down the center and laid flat side up. The underside must be a sight to behold."

"Funny, how it looks all wrong for the room," Melody Bainbridge said, "and at the same time, completely . . ."

"Right." In exact unison, they said the word.

"Do you really think so?" Blanche sounded surprised. "I was just thinking that the room would look much better with a lovely big rug."

Dunstan spread his hands and shrugged. "The wood was covered once. Called the Matted Gallery, it was. Wall-to-wall rush matting it had to soften footsteps and even out the room's appearance."

"Our good fortune it was removed," his Melody murmured, leaning down to run a gloved finger across the uneven surface. "I find a touch of the sublime in these knotted and grained rough-hewn planks set down in the midst of so much that is polished and perfect."

She waved at the rest of the room, her words in harmony with his thoughts. "Aye, beneath most o' life's pretty veneers lies a bit of ugliness, crudeness, and one can only hope, a good measure of strength."

The veil swung in his direction. He heard Melody's swift intake of breath. "Would you compare me to a floor, sir?"

"I would," he said honestly.

"Well, I will not be walked on!" she snapped, offended, when he had no intention to offend.

So out of keeping was her defensive posture to his own complimentary stance that Dunstan laughed, which only served to affront her further.

They did not part on the best of terms.

Chapter Seven

Tunbridge Wells, Kent, November 1820

In the course of the following few days, Melody planned any number of outings and excursions, galvanized by the fire of her anger. It was an emotion first lit by Mr. Hay's insolence at Knole. The Duchess of Dorset unknowingly stoked it to bonfire heights along with the Guy Fawkes offering that was three days in rising on the green.

Why? Because she did not see fit to invite either Melody or her cousin Blanche to a ball to be given in honor of her guest, the Earl of Erroll. The bonfire and the ball were the talk of the town, the former because it was to be the best and biggest ever burned, the latter largely due to the inflammatory suggestion that the earl meant to appear in full Highland regalia.

Melody pretended not to suffer the slight of her exclusion from the second of these prospective activities as she arranged transport, letters of entry, and access to suitable inns for sustenance in and along the roads to several excursions. She was not to be heard muttering aloud above one or two times, "Stupid ball. I did not want to go to it anyway. We have, after all, never been introduced to either the earl or the duchess."

It was only that mention of the sensational Earl of Erroll, and kilts, reminded her of the rude Mr. Hay. She wondered briefly how the gardener would look wearing such garb—if he was gardener at all. She was not convinced.

"Like a floor, indeed!" she muttered to herself. "And a damaged one at that! The nerve of the man!"

She took her cousin to the baths, that they might steep themselves in hot water and steam. No matter that three elderly matrons splashed their way out of the dipping pool as soon as they splashed in. No matter that they saw a roan horse in the street as they were leaving.

To the Church of King Charles the Martyr they went arm in arm, squeezing themselves into a pew with a stoutish gentleman and his even more portly wife, who gave them the cut direct in moving at once to another section, where she stood frowning and waving at her husband until he figured out that she meant him to join her.

Melody pretended not to notice, certainly not to care, though she kept her face upturned to the ceiling, less to gawk at Doogood's beautiful plasterwork than to discourage a spate of unexpected tears from splashing onto the pages of her psalter.

To Tonbridge and Hever castles they traveled, and Bayham Abbey and High Rocks just south of the town for a nuncheon alfresco.

An alfresco fiasco. And why? Because of Mr. Hay of course. For on that day, as had been the case with every other day, as if he were in some way informed of their itinerary, they encountered none other than the offensive and insulting gardener. Daily they had the misfortune to bump into him: on the Bath House steps, in the promenade, along the road, at the lighting of the bonfire itself, where he made a point of speaking to them. He sat in the vacated pew beside them in chapel, tipped his hat at the lending library, stopping each time just long enough to exchange a few pleasantries, to wish them a good day, to ask after their health.

He did not apologize for his insult, did not act as if he were guilty of even the slightest offense—behaved, in fact, as if they were on the most cordial of terms.

"The man is everywhere we go," Melody complained to Blanche in the carriage they had hired on the day they drove to Bayham Abbey. It was not so much the man she minded, as the feeling she was watched and followed.

"Who, dear?"

"Mr. Hay."

"Indeed he is," Blanche agreed. "I have grown quite fond of the sight of him. He is very polite, very kind. Do you not agree?"

"I do not." Melody gazed blindly at the passing countryside. "He has never apologized for a remark that quite offended me."

"That flooring thing? It was a compliment, my dear. Did he not say he was quite taken with it? He never intended to offend you. I am convinced. He is ever all that is polite."

"Too polite. Too kind. What does he want of us?"

"Want? Why should he want anything?"

"Do you not, as a rule, find that men are in the habit of wanting something?"

Blanche assumed a puzzled expression. "But what would Mr. Hay want of us? I feel it is we who benefit from his appearances, his connections."

"Connections? The connections of a gardener?"

"Yes. We should never have had such an enjoyable day at Knole without his freedom to roam about the place, and I have good reason to believe he is in some way connected to the Earl of Erroll. Perhaps he can obtain us an invitation to the ball at Knole."

"But what has the Earl of Erroll to do with our Mr. Hay?"

"Scotsmen, my dear. They are both Scotsmen. I think it very probable they have traveled down from the Highlands together."

"And you hope to gain introduction to the earl by way of his gardener?"

"I am not convinced the man is a gardener. I do not know many gardeners so well read in history and architecture as is our Mr. Hay."

Melody was loath to admit that the very same thought had crossed her mind.

"Whoever he may be," Blanche said, "there are not so very many in Tunbridge Wells who go out of their way to acknowledge us in the street, to offer every appearance, too, of being glad of the encounter."

It was too true, a painful verity. Melody could not admit, even to herself, that she began to feel disappointed when a day passed without Mr. Hay showing himself. She was not at all ready to admit she spent some time each morning anticipating just when and where they would encounter the gentle-voiced gardener. He was just leaving Hever Castle as they arrived, just arriving at Tonbridge as they left, and scrambling about the weather-carved sandstone outcroppings of High Rocks when they spread their picnic lunch.

"I do not see the lion in it," she was saying to Blanche when who should step from behind the crouched rock but Mr. Hay, saying in his distinctive Scottish burr, "More rabbit to the shape of it than lion. Would you no' agree?"

"A very big rabbit," Blanche said.

"Is it the rock or yourself you refer to, Mr. Hay?" Melody asked.

He smiled. "The rock, o'course. For if creature I be, it is neither rabbit nor lion I am most likened to."

"What then?"

"Will you no' take a guess?"

Recalling her first impression of him, for he wore much the same outfit then as he did today, Melody blurted without thinking, " 'Tis not a creature at all, but a bird you resemble. A falcon, I think."

Head tilting, he made a little nod of acquiescence. "Just so," he said.

Blanche asked him if he cared to join them in partaking of a bite of nuncheon. "So much food have we brought, after all, that we could not possibly consume the whole of it ourselves."

"I think not." He studied Melody, veiled as she was,

for her reaction. "I do not think Lady Bainbridge would care to share her meal with a bird o' prey, any more than the lords care to pass judgment on their queen."

"There was a vote today, was there not?" Blanche asked, highly interested.

"Aye, but so small was the margin between those who found her guilty and those who did not that another vote is to be cast."

Melody pretended, of course, to be interested in his talk of the queen, in coaxing him to stay and take a bite with them. She went so far as to lie when he asked her, rather awkwardly, if she would not prefer to be left alone, that she might remove her veil and enjoy the breeze, enjoy eating without netting getting in the way. And she lied as he took his leave of them, when he asked without any polish or refinement, if she was angry with him.

"I am inclined to think you must be in some way put out with me, Lady Bainbridge, so quiet have you been today."

"Not at all." She fixed her gaze not on Mr. Hay, but on the road behind him. In the distance a man on horseback was to be seen, a roan horse that sent fear coursing through her by no more reason than its color. "Whatever reason would I have for being put out with you?"

"I do not know," he admitted. "But I would feign have it in the open if you are, that we might make peace, whatever the trouble may be."

Of course she could not tell him, could not point to a distant rider and name her irrational fears, her sense of despair, of loss, of heartache.

To Blanche she said only, "I thought him very rude," when her cousin commented on his appearance the following morning. Her list of fears seemed all the more foolish, all the more unmentionable, amid the comfortingly familiar smell of tea and toast and marmalade.

"I was very much looking forward to the prospect of spending an afternoon out of doors without that dratted veil to block the breeze," she said. "There was no method by which I could pass food to my mouth with any great success, and no sooner does he discommode me than Mr. Hay rushes away again. He made no attempt to engage me in any conversation, though it would seem he had a great deal that was private to discuss with you."

"He realized he inconvenienced you, my dear, and went away because of it," Blanche said.

Unconvinced, Melody stabbed at the yolk of her egg. Bright yellow, it bled onto the plate.

"He told me as much, Melody, but I can see you are in no mood to be charitable toward him, or his motivations, though I cannot understand why you should be determined to take him into dislike."

Melody sighed, catching sight of her bruised reflection in the gilded mirror hung just behind the tea table, where they ate on trays brought up to them by the landlady. Displeased, she peered at the broken egg on her plate instead. "Do forgive me, Blanche," she said very quietly, "but I am inclined to take all men into dislike at present."

Blanche, busily scraping toast, a trifle too done, seemed not to hear her. "I cannot understand, either, why you should lie to him outright when he asked if you were in any way angry with him."

Melody shrugged. "One must lie, surely, under such circumstances? It would be most impolite, too outspoken, not to."

"Too outspoken?" Blanche ceased her scraping. "But Melody, your candor is one of the sensibilities I cherish most in you. You do not go to the trouble to render yourself overly polite to me, do you?"

"No. Of course not!" Melody, anticipating her needs, passed her the butter. "I make every effort to be open with you, Blanche, and honest of my feelings."

"Why should Mr. Hay deserve any less?"

Melody toyed with her egg. She was not really hungry, but if she spread her food about the plate a little and took an occasional bite, Blanche would not trouble her in insisting she must eat, nor remind her she was falling away to skin and bone, so little did she bother to consume. "He is a stranger to me, and a man, and men do not care to be burdened with a woman's outspokenness very often. It only serves to make them . . ."

"What, my dear?"

Melody stared at her fork full of food as if it were a foreign object. "Do you hear what I am saying?" she asked the egg, as if it could give answer.

Blanche looked up from the marmalade, puzzled. "But of course I hear you."

Melody carefully set aside her fork, pushing back the plate of food as if it disgusted her. "Those were Burke's thoughts, Burke's words! I had no idea they were still trapped in my head. He was always telling me I had driven him to strike me, by way of my outspokenness."

"Oh, my dear," Blanche exclaimed sympathetically, reaching out to pat her hand. "Burke's abuse of you had, I think, very little to do with what you said, or how you said it, and very much to do with the man's evil need to strike out at something or someone weaker than he. But, my dear, he controls you still if your behavior is in any way modified because of his cruelties to you."

Melody planted elbows impolitely on the table and cradled her bruised head between her hands, laughing bitterly. "God, what a fool I was to trust him, to trust in any man."

"Ah. Well, then. I do not suppose you will be much inclined to trust Mr. Hay's offer. He sends us an invitation," Blanche said quietly.

"Invitation?" Melody looked up from a study of crumbs. In that single word she could hear her own loneliness. With an agitated flick of the wrist she transferred a few of the larger crumbs to her plate. "What? Do not tell me he finagles us an invitation to the Duchess of Dorset's ball?"

"No. But Mr. Hay asked me yesterday if we would care to accompany him to Penshurst Place. He goes there the day after tomorrow to collect more fruit trees."

"He wishes us to watch him dig up saplings?" she scoffed, growing more impatient of the crumbs by the minute.

"No. He said we would be free to tour the Great Hall while he is otherwise engaged. That he will arrange for the Sidney's housekeeper to show us about."

"Oh?" Melody looked up, caught sight of her reflection again, and frowned. "Mr. Hay wishes not to see the house with us?"

"Evidently not. Perhaps he has seen it already. Perhaps he would keep his distance from a young lady who bristles like a hedgehog whenever he is about."

Melody threw her napkin over the crumbs, that they might no longer worry her. "Am I so offensive, Blanche?"

The napkin had an egg stain, a blot as ugly as her reflection, as ugly, perhaps, as her recent behavior toward Mr. Hay.

Blanche went on as if she did not hear the question. "He did mention that he would bring along a basket of provisions. Even made a point of saying he would absent himself while we were eating, that you might remove your veil and take sustenance in comfort."

"He said that?" This bit of news distracted her.

"He did. I thought it very considerate, but you will, perhaps, insist on finding something rude or offensive even in kindness?"

Melody rose abruptly, crumbs forgotten, egg stains no longer important. "Blanche, have I been so very hateful, so completely perverse?"

Blanche looked at her sadly. "You have of late, been less than tolerant of anything to do with gentlemen, and while you have good reason to harbor ill feelings toward one gentleman in particular, I think it an injustice to assume all men equal in their capacity for evil. How shall I answer Mr. Hay?"

Chapter Eight

Penshurst, Kent, November 7, 1820

The drive to Penshurst Place, in a well-sprung, unmarked, open carriage drawn by two sturdy, if unmatched horses should have been pure joy. The day was fine, the country passed through marked in the most picturesque fashion with hop farms, ost houses, orchards, and sandstone outcroppings. The company was cheerful, and yet Melody was not completely happy with their progress.

A lone rider on a roan horse took the same road they did, and as if to confirm her cousin's feeling that Mr. Hay kept his distance because of her poor opinion of him, he spent almost the entire time talking to Blanche. Upon their arrival at Penshurst Place, he took himself away with an almost unseemly haste. Melody suffered an insecurity of feelings, felt in some way outcast, unwanted and estranged—feelings she was well familiar with, but not in context with Mr. Hay.

The house, all red roofs and crenellated sandstone, was almost of a size with Knole. A little more scattered in its construction, as were her thoughts without Mr. Hay to serve as guide, the wandering wings of the place were entered by way of the Great Hall, barnlike in both size and proportion. It was a hall of the old style, with an open hearth in its center and nothing so decorative as its high, chestnut-timbered ceiling. Melody's first impression of this, the heart of the house, was of a room, cold, bare, and echoing—a lonely place, little changed by time, not at all welcoming. A mirror image of her own heart.

She did not care for it.

Following Blanche and the housekeeper thereafter, a little dazedly, through the armlike wings of Penshurst, Melody found herself drawn, time and again, to windows. She looked out over the road for the roan horse. This was not so surprising a diversion. Most of the house was only a single room in width. Every room overlooked the lane, gardens, deer park, or grounds.

More than furnishings and wall hangings, Melody enjoyed the neatly shaped arrangement of ornamental shrubs, the even rows of fruit trees, the hard-edged geometric shapes of several small knot gardens. She enjoyed, too, the glimpses to be had of Mr. Hay in the garden, his rolled-up shirtsleeves gleaming white in the sunlight.

In observing the man thus from a distance, Melody realized how much she missed his companionship—his diverting tales of past scandal and intriguing personalities, his incisive banter and stinging repartee. He had, for a short time, reminded her that she was alive, that she had much to offer in opinion if not in status or worldly goods.

To be sure, the Hall's housekeeper was informative. A great many improvements had been made over the years to Penshurst. Mrs. Edwards proudly detailed each and every one, as well as identifying by name and title all of the Sidney family members who had deigned to sit for a portrait.

The house seemed a lifeless corpse hung with the faces of a hundred lifeless corpses, until, with one more painted face pointed out to her, Melody dared ask, "Sir Philip Sidney. Was he not the Sidney who refused water that was offered him while he lay dying on a battlefield?"

"He was, marm!" The housekeeper seemed pleased she should recognize him. "Too good for this world was Sir Philip."

"I have never encountered such a man."

"Would that they were all such as he. Seven hundred mourners followed his funeral procession, poor, dear Sir Philip. Buried like a king, he was."

Another portrait was pointed out, this one of a well-dressed woman surrounded by six, stiff, doll-like girls dressed in the same formal, high-collared Elizabethan style.

"The Lady Sidney and six of her fine children. Dear woman, she and good Sir Robert, Philip's brother, took over when poor Philip's life was cut short. A wealthy Welsh heiress, her dowry rendered possible many of the improvements made by Sir Robert during her lifetime. A most excellent and treasured woman."

"She was certainly prolific," Blanche said blandly.

"Indeed, that she was, and knew well how to manage both her children and her household. Clever lady! She oversaw everything to do in the house and gardens while her husband was away at court."

"Was Sir Robert aware of his good fortune in possessing such a wife, or had she pleased him enough in bringing to him her fortune?" Melody asked skeptically, crossing to the window.

The housekeeper laughed. "No fortune hunter, our Robert, never fear. Devoted to her, he was, dear man. In all of the letters he wrote her from court, he addressed her as his sweetheart or his dear Barbara. She sent him baskets of fruit from his treasured gardens, and he sent her wines and cheeses, meat pies, and trinkets. He indulged her with gifts and freedoms no end, and trusted her in all things."

"A fortunate female," Melody said, regarding with more than a twinge of envy the bounds of the beautiful property the stiffly posed woman and her abundance of daughters had inhabited. Such a life she had imagined for herself, such dreams she had dared dream. Lost now, all of it, lost forever.

On the road a roan, and on the roan a man, the sight of whom set her heart racing. Damn Burke! So much had he stolen from her—must he steal peace of mind, too? She shook her head and turned her back on the rider. She must divorce herself from her fear of roan horses as much as ever she divorced herself from the dream of living in a grand house like Penshurst.

"A pity, my dear, is it not," Blanche quietly voiced, joining her at the window, "that Burke could not more closely have resembled Robert Sidney? I know it must pain you more than a little, cousin, to think there is no such future in store for you."

Melody regarded Blanche, astonished. So obvious and painful were the truths her cousin expressed that they were only made more painful in having found voice. "And you, Blanche?" she asked with sudden insight. "Does it pain you that you have no children? That your union with Edward was cut short? That the house and grounds went to his brother's family?"

As though stung, Blanche's eyes flew wide. She shook her head, looking about her a trifle stunned before saying, "I cannot regret anything in connection with my dear Edward, no matter how brief. As for children . . ." She waved her hand, as if to brush away the matter. "I have my nieces and nephews, and as much as I adore them, I enjoy sending them home to their parents. I do not think I would have made a very good parent."

"No?"

"Not without Edward beside me."

Melody forced herself to face the roan on the road once again. It was just a horse, and on the horse a man, no more threatening or fearsome than other men. Softly she said, "I think I would have liked to have had children."

Blanche did not appear to hear. "I cherish my memories," she said, her words overriding Melody's. "And live quite comfortably in my little cottage, and rather than while away my hours alone—so like are our circumstances—I could not bear to think of your going anywhere else to live."

Were they like? Melody saw some small difference

between a loving marriage ended by the misfortune of death, and a loveless marriage rent asunder by violence and incompatibility. "It was kind of you to ask me to stay with you," she said faintly, regretting her indebtedness to Blanche. No matter how graciously offered, it was her cousin's charity she depended upon.

"I am so pleased you have agreed to see to the details and comforts of my life."

Blanche's every utterance seemed designed to add salt to her wounds.

"Your hardships remind me that I am not the only female who struggles to survive."

Melody laughed. "Glad to serve some purpose," she said wistfully.

"Odd." Blanche linked their arms at the elbow, regarding her for a moment, through her netting, as if confused.

"Am I?" Melody grew more amused by the moment.

"Decidedly!" Blanche seemed perplexed "I always imagined, Melody, that you and your talents were destined for far greater things."

Melody had no ready quip with which to respond. Behind the veil, behind cheerful denials and assertions of contentment, she hid great depths of disillusionment and despondency. She had made her bed—in marrying Burke, in choosing now to divorce him. Nothing left, but to lie in it.

Chapter Nine

She was quiet today, the Lady Bainbridge. He might have said withdrawn or despondent, had Dunstan been able to better gauge her expression. But the veil—the bloody, irritating mystery of her veil—shut the truth of her away from him.

Dunstan was used to reading people, observing their expressions as a means to understanding mind, heart, even temperament. He could not read Lady Bainbridge. She was an unopened book to him, a haunting, unsung Melody. The longer he went without turning her pages, without clear and telling notes to sound upon the sensitive inner recesses of his ears, the more he dwelt on the fading memory of what he had seen of her.

He yearned for answers, yearned selfishly to tear away her veil, to talk to her intimately of her unfortunate connection to Lord Bainbridge. Only once before had Dunstan suffered such an unquenchable thirst. And Gillian had gulped down like honeyed mead sipped on the sly from another man's cup. Could he but wet his throat with some sense of Lady Bainbridge, another sweet spirit not his to drink, he was sure she would lose all allurement, all distraction to his thoughts and senses. He could leave this lush, gentle, rolling countryside for the lonely mist-hung toars and frowning corries of home, content and reaffirmed in the soundness of his chosen solitude, his bachelorhood.

He enjoyed his solitary morning in the Penshurst orchards and gardens. Plants distracted him from growing seeds of thought and feeling that threatened to break the surface of a calm he had maintained for going on three years, a calm he had striven hard to maintain after Gillian had broken his heart in refusing him.

Apricots, peaches, cherries, and plums thrived in a lush abundance not to be witnessed in the colder, thin-soiled north. That only cherries, beans, cauliflower, cabbages, carrots, and a few hazelnut tree seedlings interested him, along with any word to be had on enriching poor soil, astounded the head gardener, who led him about and sent pot boys scampering to serve his needs.

Dunstan was astounded himself at his impulse to invite Lady Bainbridge and the Blanche creature to accompany him today. He was impatient with his own distractedness. His gaze kept straying to the windows of Penshurst Place. His thoughts centered not on the correct identification of beans and seed potatoes, of which he was procuring samples, knobby, red-skinned, and blue, but on the afternoon ahead, when he would have the chance once again to speak to Lady Bainbridge. He had been tongue-tied at sight of her in the drive to Penshurst, unsure of himself, because he knew his presence at High Rocks had proved so unwelcome.

He worried over the suitability of the provisions he had brought with him. He had little idea as to what women cared to eat. He had never made it a point to study such things. There had been little need.

He had not heard her laugh of late, that wonderful captivating laugh. Rarely in his presence did she so relax. That troubled him.

It was Melody Bainbridge who came to fetch him from among his seeds when the ladies were done with their tour. Like a pale, hooded beekeeper she looked, or a nun. The first words were hers.

"Tell me, Mr. Hay, about your beans."

Hesitantly—he was not sure she did not ask the question facetiously—he recovered his thoughts to explain. "Beans will grow in Scotland."

"Oh? Nothing else?" Again, he could not be sure if her interest was genuine.

"Little else. The soil is poor."

"I had heard you produce large crops of barley and oats."

She surprised him. "Aye," he said warily. "Some few turnips, kale, cauliflower, carrots, and potatoes, too."

"No fruit?"

"Some berries. The brambles are hardy enough. Much of the rest cannot withstand our winters. We have had some luck with trees, though fruit trees, soft as they are, will most likely perish." Fruit trees and bruised young women, he thought, impatient with his own preoccupation with the hot house exotic he was sure hid beneath a veil, laughing at him and his beans.

"Are you forced to do a great deal of your plantings in hot beds, and under cover of bell jars, cloches, or cold frames?" she asked, a prod to continue her amusement he supposed, until she spoke quite knowledgeably of trenching the soil and asked what sort of fertilizers he preferred.

That she found his mention of seaweed, wool waste, and fish guano a matter of interest, soon had him babbling about the inherent properties of dung, bone, blood, horn, and hoof until his own words sounded ridiculous to him, and he stopped short, to apologize, saying, "I do beg your pardon, Lady Bainbridge. Such topics, perhaps, offend a lady's more delicate sensibilities."

"Not at all," she said briskly. "Why should a woman not speak as freely as a man about land and its improvement?"

He chuckled. What a baffler she continued to be. "No reason at all," he said, though he had, until today, never encountered such a woman. "If someone does but take the time to teach her, given she has a bit o' good sense and the desire to learn."

"Most women, I have found, sir, have a great deal

more sense than the world would credit them with. As for desire . . ." She paused.

Dunstan raised his brows and tried to stop his mouth from twitching. "No need to be telling me women have a great deal more desire than the world would credit them with."

"Neither need, nor the intention, Mr. Hay. I had a desire to learn about land, and my father taught me. He was possessed of some acreage and instructed me in everything about it that he might have taught the son he never had. He believed women were every bit as sensible as men, some more so."

"I see. I would've liked to have met such a man. He is gone now, is he? Or do I overstep my bounds in asking?"

She was silent a moment, the veil guarding her reaction. "He died when I was married but two months." Her voice sounded choked. "My mother, dispossessed of husband, child, and her home of many years, died very unhappy, not long after."

"So sorry."

"Yes. Of course." The words were bitter.

"And the land?"

The bitterness intensified. "Where else, but in my uncle's care? He has sons who will inherit when he is gone."

"Have you no garden, then, in which to get your hands dirty and remember—"

"What has slipped through my fingers for no more reason than my sex?" she interrupted.

"Uhm, noo, I was going to say . . . your father?"

"Oh." She laughed a little. He reveled in its brief spurt. "I beg your pardon," she said, grown serious again. "I find myself out of sorts of late."

"But o'course you do," he said. "Tell me, do you mean to attend the ball at Knole? There is nothing like a bit o' music and a dance or two to lift the spirits."

"I do like to dance, but we will not be attending."

"No?" He managed to instill that single word with

a great deal of disappointment. "Do you mind my asking, whyever not?"

"That is the problem, you see. We were not asked to attend."

"Not asked?" He frowned, shrugged, and smiled at her. "Perhaps the invitation has only gone astray."

He led them through the gatehouse, footsteps echoing, stopping when they emerged on the other side, in the drive that led through the deer park.

"Whose horse?" Lady Bainbridge asked, her voice fainter than usual.

Dunstan, who leaned into the carriage by which he had brought them, leaned out again to study a sleek, saddled roan that stood switching flies beside his bays. "I've no idea. Another guest I suppose." He said it absently as he handed out several baskets, which they divided between them before setting off across the open park for a stand of trees on rising ground.

He would have given no further thought to the horse, had not Lady Bainbridge, veil flowing, turned more than once to look back at it, her manner as skittish as the grazing roe deer who lifted gracefully antlered heads at their approach. A few loped away.

"Do you mind me asking, Mrs. Claybourne, my Lady Bainbridge"—Dunstan's head swiveled first one way and then the other, for they walked three abreast along a narrow track that skirted the neighboring churchyard, in which neat rows of headstones had been planted—"what would home be meaning to the two of you?"

"I do not mind you asking, Mr. Hay," Lady Bainbridge said. The breeze, unblocked by architecture or trees, filled her mouth with netting, which made her sound muffled rather than sharp in saying, "I do mind hearing myself styled Lady Bainbridge when it is that title of which I strive so valiantly to rid myself."

He would like to free her of the veil. "What shall I be calling you then, marm?" He took a basket from her that she might more easily fend off windblown netting.

"Not marm, if you please," she said, throwing yet another glance behind her. "Does it feel to you as if the house watches us from here?" she asked.

Dunstan turned to look at the house. There was the sensation that they might be watched from any of the windows that faced the track they walked. "Aye," he said. The sensation diminished as the track curved to the left past a beautifully sodded and fenced-off square that appeared to be maintained as a bowling green.

Blanche filled the silence that Melody Bainbridge made no effort to fill, politely suggesting, "I would suppose there is nothing for it, Mr. Hay, but that you must feel free to call us Blanche and Melody."

He did his best to sketch a bow, with both arms heavily laden. "Blanche and Melody it is, and far merrier names than Claybourne and Bainbridge, if you don't mind me saying so. Will you be kind enough to reciprocate?"

"I think not, Mr. Hay," Melody Bainbridge responded coolly, reaching to take her basket from his hand in so unexpected a move he hung onto the thing for a moment, stunned by her proximity, by a perfume-laden whiff of spices and citrus.

"I've no objection," Blanche contradicted her even as Melody said irritably, "Let go, Mr. Hay. I can well manage the thing. You carry too much of the burden as it is."

"Very kind," he said, releasing the handle. "You were telling me your definition of home?"

"Was I? Well, surely my concept of home must be much the same as anyone else's." She struggled with her veil again.

"Must it?" Their path led them past a line of elm trees, taller and straighter than those in Scotland. "Perhaps you will agree with me that home is not so much place as it is a feeling of safety, of dominion, of rootedness. Cave, castle, or cottage—a place where all o' the lions of life can be held at bay . . ."

"Mmm. Very eloquent, sir. I suppose I would agree with that assessment, but home to me is also a place of complete comfort and relaxation, a place to take the pins from one's hair."

"Aye." He stared at her veil and tried to remember what her hair looked like at all, much less what it might look like unpinned. "And the veil from one's head."

His response made Blanche interject hastily, "And the shoes from one's feet."

Dunstan did his best not to imagine that scenario.

"You say place is not important?" Melody Bainbridge's voice held an unmistakable challenge.

"You disagree?" Why was he not surprised?

"I do," she said. "Home to me is more bird's nest than cave. It is feathered exactly to one's taste. At home one may surround oneself with all that pleases—colors, patterns, textures, even people."

"I suppose, though at present my home is more indicative of my ancestor's tastes than my own."

"Family does imprint itself on a home inhabited by generations," Blanche said wisely.

"Aye."

"Will you tell me of your home?" Lady Bainbridge asked. He could not stop thinking of her in such terms.

"My wee place in the country? Or do you mean Scotland? Home in the larger sense?"

"Both, if you please." She sounded genuinely interested, as she had in discussing gardening technique.

He licked his lips, strangely reluctant to tell her. Hay Hall was not a place, he thought, to impress this English rose. He took a deep breath. "'Tis a lonely site, my home, but so bonnie it takes my breath away. A house not so grand as Knole or Penshurst, drafty and old, made of the local stone, in need of updating, but a sturdy place of some antiquity, built where the mountains meet the plains in Aberdeen district."

"A farm, is it?"

"There is farming thereabout. A rude style o' tenant farming unchanged since medieval times—clachans and crofters, foot plow and little in the way of replenishing the soil."

"And you would change that?"

"I would. In my own little corner of the world, anyway. It is a pretty place for all that it is a wee bit backward. There are two rivers nearby, the Don and the Dee, and as backdrop the misty, flat-topped heights of the Grampian and Cairngorm mountains. It is a place perfumed by pine, heather, and snow. Eagles soar above the peaks. Capercallies croak in the woods. Deer, such as these"—a trio of tiny, red roe deer trotted fearlessly alongside them for a moment—"run free and wild."

"It is plain you love the place," she said quietly.

"I cannot imagine living out my years anywhere else. Stay a moment." Dunstan stopped to dig enthusiastically into one of the baskets he carried.

"What are you looking for?" Blanche asked. "May we be of any assistance?"

"Corn," he said. "I am told the deer here are tame enough to hand feed."

Blanche rooted in her basket. "I do not see anything that looks like corn."

"A burlap bag," he said.

"Is this it?"

Dunstan was at Melody's side in an instant, relieving her of her basket, pulling out the bag. "Remove your gloves, ladies." He dragged his own free with the aid of his teeth. "Swiftly now! The deer have determined we mean to feed them."

Indeed, the dainty creatures moved in far more aggressively than Melody would have imagined. Smaller than they seemed from a distance, the tallest males' shoulders were no higher than her waist, but the horns above their sweetly attenuated noses added a certain fierceness to their diminutive scale. The does seemed somehow underdressed without racks to adorn their heads, while the fawns, smallest of all, roan red coats darkening for winter, hung shyly back from the press, black-rimmed ears twitching.

"Hold out your hands," Mr. Hay directed, dumping a handful of corn into Blanche's palms, sprinkling more on the ground at her feet, moving quickly to fill Melody's hands as the deer pressed forward, bumping shoulders in their eagerness, snorting and grunting like dainty limbed pigs.

"How wonderful!" Blanche chortled from above a sea of waving horns and tossing heads.

Not wonderful at all, Melody thought as kernels of corn, hard, dry, and yellow—strange coinage—overfilled her palms. Too many, they spilled from her fingers. She could not control the loss of them.

"No more," she said, even as Dunstan Hay tried to help, one of his hands cupping beneath the spill of gold, his fingers brushing her knuckles.

Melody had not been touched in any way by man or beast for so long she gasped as the deer shoved against her like hungry colts, nervy enough to test her offering, stepping in to butt muzzles against her hands, her arms, her hips. Their breath was warm and fast and moist. Kernels of corn crunched and ground in the black-banded mouths. Impatient and thrusting, the weight of a velvet muzzle pushed her hands into Mr. Hay's palm as he maneuvered out of the way of the anxious feeders, his hand continuing to cup hers.

She panicked and backed into him as he pivoted to stand behind her. The sensation of velvety, behaired lips feeding from her palms was unexpectedly provocative. The warm resistance of a man's chest and thighs briefly pressing her back and buttocks as his hand clasped hers, took her breath away. The harbor of his arm shifted to encompass her waist, the better to pour another flood of rough, dry pellets.

Gall rose in her throat, her mouth made bitter as one of the bucks, impatient to feed, rose to plant hooves briefly on her shoulders.

Unprepared for the sudden weight, she shrieked

and jerked back. Corn went flying. Her veil whirled. Ramming into Mr. Hay's chest, her knees buckled. He caught her when she might have fallen, his hands firmly clasping her shoulders, his body cushioning hers, back, buttocks, and thighs, absorbing the brunt of the deer's impact. His voice rose to frighten away the greedy animal.

"Away wi' you, unmannerly beastie."

The buck jumped back, forcing the others to fall away. The deer were far less cowed by Mr. Hay's hand than Melody was. His voice in her ear, the vibration of each word, the rise and fall of his chest against her back, added to her panic. Her pulse thundered. Her every muscle tensed.

"Not afeered of them, are you?" he asked as she jerked herself upright, leapt from the alarming cradle of his arms, smoothed her skirts, and adjusted the fall of her veil with trembling hands.

Big-eyed innocence, the deer snuffled the grass at her feet, searching for additional handouts.

"No." She tried to laugh away her exaggerated anxiety. "Merely unprepared for such an excess of a-a-affection," she stammered.

"Not so much affection as greed from this lot," he contended.

"Of course. Quite right. One ought not confuse the two," she agreed.

Blanche joined them, her color high, her cap knocked askew. "A strange sensation that. Their lips, their teeth, in my hand."

Mr. Hay nodded. "Unexpectedly hairy, are they no'?"

"They are," she agreed.

He dusted off his palms and shot a look Melody's way. "Enough of that then."

"Ready to proceed, are we?" Blanche sounded disappointed.

"There is more corn if you'd prefer to stay a bit longer." Mr. Hay offered her the bag.

"No, no," Blanche said. "I would feed myself now."

They progressed along a small rise, the deer trailing hopefully, to a secluded stand of oak trees in the shade of which Dunstan suggested they stop to eat their picnic, a grand view of Penshurst before them.

Melody was pleased she was no longer required to suppress her panic as much as her windblown veil, pleased to see Mr. Hay lead the deer away with the promise of the last of the corn and a handful of salt.

A ground cloth was spread, the baskets unpacked, a bottle of wine uncorked. They arranged themselves on three corners of the cloth, the food between them, simple fare but filling—meat pasties, cucumber sandwiches, a wedge of cheddar, a loaf of pumpernickel, a basket of freshly picked pippins, and a tin full of ratafia cakes.

"Do you mean to drink and eat behind that thing?" Dunstan Hay asked flatly when Melody took a cup from his hand, the moving shadows of the treetops overhead throwing shifting patterns on the netted surface of her veil.

"I do," she said, still shaken, more in need of her shield than ever.

"Suit yourself." He sat looking at her, as if he saw straight through the veil, through her unfounded mistrust of him to the core of her damaged confidence. "I've no desire to make you uncomfortable. It just looks as if it gets in the way."

"I've grown quite adept at doing things with it on."

He shrugged, filled her cup, and another for Blanche, saying over his shoulder, "I'm sure you have, but there's no real need if you'd prefer to feel the breeze. We will not be disturbed, and . . ."

"And?"

He stood, the neck of the wine bottle dangling from a two-fingered hold, to gaze up the hill. "And I will take a wee walk that you might do so, if you should desire the privacy."

Beneath the veil, she frowned. "I am fine, really."

"Are you then? I will admit I had just as soon stay and talk."

"No need to leave, sir."

"No, none at all," Blanche seconded.

"I have not made myself clear." He sank down on the ground cloth again, the wine bottle between them, his thumb catching a drop or two of liquid that spilled. The thumb carried the wine to his mouth, focusing her attention too completely on his lips.

Uneasily, she checked the arrangement of her skirt. "You are kind to concern yourself with my comfort."

"Nay," he said, his gaze keen. "It is selfish, I am."

"Selfish?" His expression concerned her more than an excess of petticoat. She had forgotten how green were his eyes, how sober his mouth.

"Aye. You see, I've a desire to see your face again, my lady, for I got no more than a wee wisp of it at the well. Enough to know I should like to see more."

"My, my. You are a plainspoken man," Blanche said nervously.

"I am that," he agreed. "It makes life easier coming straight to the heart o' things, rather than skirting round them. But as I've said"—he addressed the remark to Melody—"I've no desire to make you uneasy. If it suits you to hide away from me, I will wait a little longer for the privilege o' looking upon your face."

Melody laughed. "I had no idea there was great privilege attached to such a thing."

"Ah." He smiled and leaned toward her, green eyes gleaming. "I have missed the sound o' that."

"Of what? Sarcasm?"

"Nay. Your laughter. 'Tis a sweet sound. The first bit o' you I had encounter with. It would seem I was meant to meet you in bits and pieces."

"Whatever do you mean?" Blanche asked.

He looked away to answer her question, and in so doing made Melody aware of how very much she enjoyed gazing into the brilliance of his eyes.

"First her laughter," he said, "then her voice, in London—yours as well. And at the waters in Tunbridge Wells, most of the remainder was exposed to me."

"Exposed?" Melody repeated sharply. As she had hoped, his attention turned once again in her direction.

"Aye. Your height, stature, and your youth, also a bit o' temper, well contained, and a sampling of courage to have faced down such an unpleasant gathering of gossipmongers without flinching. Then you showed me your face, and in showing it, shamed me."

"Shamed you, Mr. Hay?" Blanche inquired.

"Aye. I had misjudged what was to be found beneath yon veil."

Melody was at the moment glad of "yon" veil, as he so quaintly put it. It hid the blush that heated cheeks uglied by bruises. It hid the face she was ashamed of. "You mentioned London?" she said.

"I did." He shifted his position on the ground cloth in reaching for an apple closer to her hand than his. She, too, shifted, that she might pass the fruit to him. Their knees, their fingers collided in the transaction.

"It was in London we first bumped into one another." He took the apple from her slowly, his gaze lingering on her hand as much as did his fingers. "Our carriages came close to it, anyway. At the parade—the brassfounder's parade. I heard you laughing."

"Eavesdropping, were you?"

He ducked his head, nodded sheepishly, and bit into the apple. "Aye," he said around his mouthful. When it was swallowed with relish, he went on. "Captured me attention, voicing me very thoughts the way you did. It was all I could do to stop myself from laughing out loud along with you, but that would have given me away." With appetite he bit again into the apple. It gave up its crisp flesh to him.

"And now you would have me give myself away?" She could not keep her eyes from his mouth as he chewed, as he suckled from the side of his hand a wayward spray of apple juice.

He joined her in laughing and waved his twice bitten apple at her. "Ironic, I suppose." The laughter brought warmth to his cheeks, brought a mischievous heat to his gaze as he said, "But do recall I have already gotten glimpse o' the damage. Come now, my lady, you've no need to hide yourself."

"Indeed," Blanche chirped.

Melody laughed again, hesitated, and then shook her head. "I am happy as I am, really."

"Are you now?" he drawled sarcastically, rising. "As happy as I am to take that stroll I mentioned. I shall not be gone much above half an hour." Munching the remains of the apple, a cheeky wink thrown her way, as if he had no doubt she watched his every move, he walked away.

Chapter Ten

He returned from his wanderings to a silence so complete he thought at first his party had abandoned the site. That two women could sit together for any length of time in complete silence never occurred to him. He was, in a way, correct in his assumption. Blanche had abandoned the ground cloth beneath the oaks, and Melody Bainbridge, her veil removed, sat propped against the trunk of one of the more substantial trees, gazing at Penshurst he thought, until he moved closer and found her not silently contemplative, but asleep.

Asleep, and in her sleep, beautiful, despite fading bruises. Careful not to wake her, wary of twigs, of acorns, of coming between her and the sun, he stepped a little closer, staring at the rise and fall of her bosom, at the gathered fabric bound by velvet ribbons beneath the sweet swell of her breasts, at the cascade of cambric puddled in her lap, at the curve of her hip, fabric drawn tight. White petticoat spilled around each slender ankle. His gaze fixed on the unexpected allure of their curves, the arch of each shoeless foot. She had removed her boots, despite the nip in the air, and set them at her side.

Closer still, breath held, he stared his fill. Pale and fragile she was, her complexion smooth as silk, her hair dove soft, fair as a new morning, her features, the pale lashes fanned against delicately rosied cheeks, all that he had remembered and more.

Tragic and out of place, her bruises had assumed a brutal blue and puce color edged in pale saffron. How could a man lift his hand against such a face? Sweet, and heart-shaped it was, flaxen tendrils kissing brows and temples, flyaway wisps fired by the dancing light of the sun as it dappled her brow. Quiet, careful, as light-footed as a fawn, he knelt beside her, enchanted—ready to eat from her hand.

A shadow! An unexpected change in the air before her face! Melody started violently. Her eyes flew wide. She inhaled with a choked gasp, her whole body stiffening with alarm. *Burke!*

Not Burke, but Dunstan Hay knelt before her, his hand paused benignly in midair, so close she could smell the soap he had used to wash his hands, the musky, cedar scent of sandalwood, the sharp tang of the grape on his breath. Possessed of more passion than his limbs, his eyes were wide, shocked. He had not expected her to fear him.

"I do beg your pardon." He lowered his hand. Soft voiced, his accent was thicker than usual. "Didna' mean to alarm you."

"What then? Creeping up on me as I slept?" Fear, anger, and humiliation coursing like fire through her veins, she turned her face from his, impatient with her own reaction, the ghost of nightmares past. She tried to remember what she had done with her veil. "It is very rude. Of course you startled me."

"O' course." He sank back on his heels, his very gaze shrinking. "Thoughtless of me. It is just . . ."

She closed her eyes, squeezing back the sudden sting of tears. She could not take his pity, could not stand to acknowledge her own ugliness, to see the ugliness of what had been done to her reflected in his eyes.

He inhaled deeply and said nothing, just loomed there at her elbow, a frightening male presence, too close for comfort.

"Just what?" she demanded, blinking her tears into submission.

"Naught really. It was just your hair . . ."

She reached up to smooth it. "Something wrong with my hair?"

"Nay. No. Not at all."

"What then? Have I a bug crawling on me? Pins coming loose?" She dared to look at him and met a gaze warm and sad and searching, emotions that reached out to her. His gaze stirred her enough that she must look away again. No pity. No contempt. None of the shocked, what-can-she-have-done-to-deserve-such-wrath sort of judgment she was used to seeing. No hint of any of that. Its very absence disturbed her.

"Nothing of the kind," he said. "It was naught but the sunlight caught up in your hair. Like spun gold it looked, a sight so fair I was quite inappropriately drawn to touching it. Do forgive me."

His voice was deep, soft, and seductive. Too well she knew the false promise of such tones.

"I thought you meant—"

"To strike you?" he said matter-of-factly.

"What? No!" She lied. His assumption angered her irrationally. "You have no reason to strike me." She said it sharply, pushing away from the tree, away from welling tears, away from his voice, his eyes, his very nearness. Rising abruptly, she turned her back on the intensity of his questioning gaze and looked out over the beauties of Penshurst, eyes misted.

"Had anyone?" he asked.

"Anyone what?"

"Reason to strike? I cannot conjure reason enough to warrant such brutality." His voice was gruff, anger thickening the strangeness of his accent. "Was he violent often?"

His candor shocked her. Overriding the anger in his voice, she thought she heard compassion. Indeed, just such a warmth of emotion burned in his gaze, knit the set of his brows, and carved the tilt of his lips. Honey sweet and golden, the weight of that look. His unexpected validation of her feelings was heart-lifting. Yet she feared being pleased with any man. She had been too easily pleased in the past, too hasty in swallowing sweet looks, sweet words, sweet, empty promises.

"That would depend on your definition of often," she said quietly.

"More than once is too often in my opinion."

"It was too often then," she agreed, forcing a laugh, forcing her tone to a lightness that in no way matched their topic.

"How can you laugh?" he asked.

She threw her head back defiantly. "I must. There is little left of me, but laughter."

Chapter Eleven

Tunbridge Wells, November 8, 1820

It rained the following day, not the sort of misting inconvenience into which one might sally forth without thought, but a chill, dreary pelting that bloomed umbrellas, splattered stockings, and rendered the country roads boggy and impassable.

The downpour put off the stroll Melody and Blanche usually made to the lending libraries every Wednesday to pick up fresh newspaper accounts of the conclusion of the king's case against his queen. The final summation had been read—the vote on the bill of Pain and Penalties taken, and yet so slim was the difference between "Content" and "Not content" that a second count had been taken and a third proposed. With such news came the latest gossip and speculation. Whispers always hung thick in Elliot's and Nash's reading rooms and along the promenade between.

"Most Gracious Queen, we thee implore . . ."

The cruel poetry was heard on everyone's lips, hushed as the rain upon the pane, a lampoon of Denman's final summation on behalf of the queen, wherein he had included Christ's wisdom to an adulterous woman,

"To go away and sin no more—
Or if that effort be too great
To go away at any rate."

It annoyed Melody to hear such malicious fun

made of an event that must pain both parties. She hoped her own case might be settled with less fanfare.

The gossips reckoned if the king's case could not find a majority among the Lords, it had scant chance in the Commons. Brougham, it was rumored, intended to bring recriminations against the king in the form of witnesses to swear to his many sexual escapades now that the queen's had been so thoroughly aired.

Locally, the Earl of Erroll had tongues wagging. He had yet to attend a local Assembly. The resident gentry had been snubbed. Few had so much as clapped eyes on the elusive gentleman. As a result, invitations to the Duchess of Dorset's ball became items even more highly prized and oft discussed. The ball promised to be the event of the season.

Melody wondered if Mr. Hay would attend; wondered, too, if Blanche was correct in assuming that Hay and the earl traveled together.

Blanche sat, pen in hand, at the secretary near the window with a lamp to brighten the gloom, attending to her correspondence. Melody hovered nearby at a little card table, playing patience, the game so boring she rose frequently to pace and stare out of the window.

She had received but one missive, and it was certainly not an invitation to the ball. Furthermore, it required no response. Her solicitor, Mr. Whitfield, informed her, most unwelcomely, that her case was still delayed by the royal proceedings. Every judge in London was occupied with the Pain and Penalties proceeding. A final vote had yet to be taken, and they did not want to rush things. The nation, certainly the courts, had little patience with the topic of divorce these days, no matter the reason. The news that her future was yet delayed did nothing to relieve the tedium of the weather. It did, in fact, leave Melody feeling restless and unsatisfied. She was ready for the business to be finished, to sever her ties to Burke—to begin anew.

"What a dreadful day," she said on more than one occasion, her mind on yesterday's picnic, on the memory of Mr. Hay's hand on hers as she fed the deer, on the moment she had opened her eyes to find him kneeling before her.

"Yesterday was lovely," Blanche said.

"It was," Melody allowed.

There was no sound thereafter for a few moments other than the scratching of Blanche's pen, the soft slap of Melody's cards, and the settling of a log in the grate.

"Have you formed an attachment for our Mr. Hay, my dear?"

The question, blandly if bluntly put, startled Melody.

"Do not be ridiculous." Impatiently, she raked the uncooperative deck into a fresh pile.

Blanche looked up from her scratchings. "You allow him to see your face, do you not?"

Awkwardly, Melody reshuffled the deck, a sticky, dog-eared pasteboard set discovered in the top drawer of her wardrobe. They had too many times been handled to fall together smoothly. "He returned from his walk to find me unveiled," she explained.

"Is that not evidence of some level of understanding between the two of you?"

Melody sniffed and cut the deck. "It seemed foolish to continue hiding once he had seen me."

"Ah," was Blanche's only response.

Row upon precise row, Melody set out the cards. Rain tapped at the pane. A clock ticked away the minutes. Burning wood crackled and popped in the fireplace. "He is, I think, discreet," she said.

Blanche did not so much as look up from her pen. "Indeed, I am sure he is. There is a gentleness about our Mr. Hay."

"Yes." The last row of cards went down as carefully as the first. "Though one can be deceived when it comes to such things."

The pen's scratching never faltered. "I do not think we are deceived in Mr. Hay."

"Are we not?" Melody studied her layout, matched what numbers she could, and turned up the ace of hearts, deuce of diamonds, and king of clubs. "We have yet to discover just who he is."

"He is Mr. Hay," Blanche said simply, as if that were enough.

"And who is Mr. Hay?" Melody abandoned her chair, restlessly crossing to the window.

"You admit then, that you wish you knew more of him?" Blanche seemed bent on vexing her, on twisting her words.

Melody tossed back the curtain, studied the course of a raindrop on the pane, scanned the misted line of rooftops that led toward the center of town. A row of disconsolate pigeons, feathers fluffed against the wet, huddled on the nearest chimney pot. "I do," she admitted, breath fogging the glass. "We spend a great deal of time in his company. It is prudence spurs my interest in whom he may be."

"Nothing more?" Blanche's pen nib clicked against the inkwell. The joints of her chair creaked as she shifted her weight. "Come now, Melody, you have been separated from your husband for two years. During that time, I have not seen you evidence the slightest interest, the remotest preoccupation, with any gentleman—not even Burke, during the recent reconciliation I am sorry to have arranged. Yet I think you are diverted by Mr. Hay."

Chilled, Melody turned her back on wet pigeons and dripping rooftops. "Diverting he may be, but I know very little about him, and I am not so foolish as to form an attachment without knowing a man thoroughly. Not a second time, cousin." Taking up the poker, she stirred the fire until sparks flew, brazen imps of heat rising from the deceptively snowy powder of ashen wood.

Blanche looked up from her letter with an arrested expression. "Knowing a man thoroughly, my dear, takes a lifetime of observation, and even then they can surprise one."

"Of that I am all too aware." Melody sighed, drew her shawl closer about her shoulders against the damp, and consigned a fresh log to the flames before returning to her game of patience.

"To be sure," Blanche said. "Is it not the potential for surprise that keeps the sexes fascinated with one another?"

Melody shrugged, tongue testing the split in her lip, now almost healed. "I am not especially fond of surprises."

"I am sorry to hear it." Blanche took up her pen again.

"Why?" The king of clubs, sword in one hand, club in the other, his painted likeness reminding her too much of Burke, blocked the progress of her play.

"We have received a most surprising invitation."

"From Mr. Hay?" Melody made every effort not to sound too eager.

"No. Though he may well be behind our receiving it. I can scarce imagine how else we have come to the attention of the Duchess of Dorset. She requests our attendance at the ball in honor of the Earl of Erroll."

Chapter Twelve

Dunstan stood in the reception line in the Great Hall at Knole, greeting arriving guests beside his hostess, scanning the crowd entering from the courtyard—blessedly dry this evening. They had feared rain might spoil attendance. Their luck, the day had been mild and none too clouded. Not a drop to muddy roads or spoil hems and hair.

A great flock of the local gentry and noble visitors to the Wells made an appearance. The announcement of their names as Dunstan shook hands again and again, ran in one ear and out the other. A few he recognized. The great majority he did not, nor did he care to. There was only one name he waited impatiently to hear.

"Is your friend arrived?" the duchess asked, brows raised, as they proceeded to the ballroom. "The one you made such a point of adding to the guest list?" Graciously, she turned to thank another of the houseguests who had participated in the reception.

"A latecomer, it would seem." He offered his arm that they might follow the young Misses Sackville toward the stairs. "I shall make a point of presenting her to you."

"Please do." She lowered her voice, slowing his progress before they entered the stairwell to confide, "Though perhaps it would be best if the girls were not made too friendly with the woman."

"Oh?" Dunstan was surprised. "Whyever not? She is perfectly respectable."

"My dear Dunstan." She patted his arm. "I would never have allowed her to set foot in my house if she were not. And I mean to make it perfectly clear she is welcome. I have every intention of introducing her to most of our guests, but I would not have my girls too well informed, if we can avoid it, on the subject of the separation." She gave his arm a squeeze. "Divorce. They need not be exposed to such an unpleasantness, need they?"

"I see," Dunstan said quietly, though in truth he did not understand the logic of her reasoning in the least. There was much a girl might learn from the failure of a marriage, was there not?

"Entrance to Knole as an invited guest," Blanche observed with a trace of excitement, "is quite a different experience from entering Knole as mere tourist. Do you not agree, Melody?"

Melody did agree as she was handed down from their hired carriage. Perhaps it was a trick of the light. The house looked bigger, more imposing. The dark bulk of walls gloomily overshadowed the gardens as dusk settled in a golden haze of light, treetops silhouetted starkly against the dying sun. In the sky, brilliant cerulean and salmon, blotted by a spreading stain of indigo, hung the pale hunter's moon. A chill edge cut the air—a shivering intensity of fogging breath, the smell of wet stone and damp leaf mold, the warm, tactile riches of evening velvets and a stiffly biting wealth of lace. The footman was mindful of the train on her dress, careful enough to point out a steaming pile of dung. Even the sound of Knole was uniquely changed. As the coachman urged the horses to walk on and they followed the lamplit path trod by a number of visitors, a high, eerie, ululating bellow trumpeted from the nearby woods.

"Did you hear that?" Blanche gasped.

"Rutting season, marm," a passing footman explained. "The bucks carry on a bit this time of year fighting over the does. If you listen carefully, you just might be able to make out the clatter of their horns." He bowed politely, leaving to welcome additional guests.

"Perhaps that explains why the little roe deer was so aggressive with you at Penshurst," Blanche suggested, plucking at Melody's sleeve.

"Perhaps," Melody agreed, her mind on other matters. "Do I look all right?" she asked, her voice echoing as they stepped through the stone gateway into the largest of Knole's courtyards.

Mindful of the reasons for her concern, Blanche stopped on the path that split the sodded green to peer at her intently in the gathering dusk.

To veil or not to veil—that was the question that had plagued Melody in dressing this evening. In the end, she had decided she would be far less conspicuous unveiled. The faint bruising still to be seen she had covered with a liberal dash of rice powder and the clever positioning of several dangling curls.

"You look lovely," Blanche said with a smile. "No one will notice a thing. Do not worry. You turn heads, my dear, not because of bruises, but because you have at last regained your looks."

Melody smiled sheepishly. "Dear Blanche. Do I plague you with my foolish sense of insecurity?"

"Never you mind." Blanche gave her hand a squeeze. "It must be strange after so many weeks safe behind your netting to go about without it. Does not Knole feel like an old friend? These wings are like great arms reaching out to enfold us."

Melody felt it, too, a sense almost of homecoming, in walking once again the Green Court, despite the growing chill and lengthening shadows, despite the chittering, swoop and dive of swallows settling to roost along the roofline. By way of the lamplit inner wicket that led beneath Bourcheir's Tower, across the smaller Stone Court, footsteps echoing, a sprinkling of guests both before and aft of them—they proceeded to the Great Hall. The dusk was alive with voices and light and the drifting strains of music.

Melody was reminded of the day they had spent exploring Knole and its beauties in the company of Mr. Hay, whom she hoped to meet once again upon the premises.

They were met at the door by a tall, liveried footman who announced them sonorously, his voice echoing from the plasterwork flowers and crosses high above their heads, "Lady Bainbridge and Mrs. Claybourne."

That detested name, a moniker she longed to be rid of, turned heads and focused all eyes in her direction. Jaws ceased working, cups halted in midgulp, all chatter briefly stilled among the guests more interested in the punch bowl and foodstuffs that graced tables stretching the length of the room than in the dancing already commenced in the ballroom above.

Melody, cheeks burning, uncertain where to look, longed for her discarded veil.

"Come along." Blanche linked an arm through hers. The hum of conversation, the clink of glasses and plate resumed in their wake. Together they proceeded to the beautiful, blessedly boxed-in Grand Staircase that had so pleased Melody on her last visit. It pleased her again, tonight. The soothingly logical progression of painted motifs, from the Age of Man below, to the Seven Virtues above, offered temporary relief from searching gazes and curious eyes. And yet, from the growing darkness of the inky sky, through diamond-paned windows high above their heads, the moon peered, a glowing, pockmarked face, almost as bright as the flickering brass-and-glass lantern that hung above the leopard newel post, watching her.

Sin lurked among the virtues in the darkness at the head of the stairs.

"Melody, sweeting, I have been waiting for you." Burke stepped from behind one of the columns. His voice, so close, the sudden, familiar rotten sugarplum reek of his cologne, so completely unexpected and unwanted, raised the hair at the base of her neck.

Melody's first, stomach-turning inclination was to vomit. Her second was to flee. Even Blanche gasped, missed her step, and almost tumbled backward down the stairs.

"Burke!" The name and all its implications sent her fear echoing down the stairwell. Melody winced at the sound of her own terror, swallowed the foul taste in her mouth, steadied Blanche by placing her palm in the small of her cousin's back, and tried her utmost to sound cool, calm, and unafraid. "I had no idea I should see you here."

"Ah, then you do remember me, my pet?" he said in his customarily sardonic tone, emerging from the shadows, his mouth arranged in a catlike smile designed to set unwary hearts aflutter.

A fine figure of a man—powerful, broad-shouldered, tightly knit, faintly leonine when he moved, Burke exuded latent danger like musky perfume. She had been lured by the power of him, by the glossy polish of his carefully constructed social facade. He had the same ready smile, the same trim figure, the same direct way of looking at her that had first convinced her he was a man among men.

Melody hated the realization that some vestige of the young woman she had once been, the naively besotted, feather-brained fool who had fallen head over heels in love with Burke Bainbridge some three years past, still thrilled to his smile. She had thought all trace of that young woman was dead. Indeed, she had worked very hard, with all that was sensible within her, to murder the bird-witted wretch. She strangled now the faint sense of communion this first sight of her husband managed to provoke. He was dressed tonight, as always, in sartorial splendor he could in no way have afforded himself. At great expense, and by the benefit of the sizable dowry she had brought to the marriage, he managed to appear magnificent in the skin-hugging black he so generally favored, topped by a sumptuous, eye-catching gold damask jacket that highlighted the subtle shine of close-cropped hair. His coloring she considered perfectly suited to a man who hid a dark coarseness under a glossy patina of elegance and refinement.

Few who met Burke and were similarly deluded would ever understand how or why Lady Bainbridge chose to leave her lord. Few would ever suffer the consequences that intimacy had won her.

"I have a little surprise for you, sweeting." His languid, purring tone set Melody's teeth on edge. Had they not been in such a public place she would have assumed he prepared to pounce on her. As it was, she knew the sealed document he drew from one of the gold jacket's capacious pockets bode ill.

"Something to read," he drawled, his glance never so much as flickering in Blanche's direction. "Something my solicitor thought your solicitor might find interesting."

She stepped past Blanche to reach for it. He whisked it away even as her fingers grazed paper. "But perhaps I will not give it to you after all. I daresay you will not find it to your taste. You are looking very well this evening, my sweet. Very well, indeed. I might be swayed to take you quietly home with me, all our past quarrels forgotten, including the dreadful business contained herein, if you will only agree with me that this foolish divorce business ought not to progress."

He toyed with her, the bird between his paws.

"Best give it to me, Burke." She held out her hand. "There is nothing you can do or say to convince me I do not wish to part forever from your company."

"Well, if you are so greedy for surprises"—with a flick of his wrist, he thrust the papers into her hands—"then you must have them."

Fearing the worst, but maintaining a surface composure, Melody broke the seal and scanned the sheets. "A countersuit!" She laughed. "Really, Burke, on what grounds?"

"Read, my dearest, read," he suggested with a smile. "It's all in there. My fellow is very thorough."

Words swam up from the mass of verbiage.

"Criminal conversation?" She laughed. "With three

mistresses of whom I am fully cognizant, you dare to accuse me? With whom am I allegedly conducting this affair?"

"Can you not guess, my pet?" he purred.

"No." She shook her head, still chuckling, the sound of it too nervous, and yet she could not be calm until the name presented itself from the page full of words. "The Earl of Erroll!" She burst out laughing, the sound high and clear, carrying from the stairwell into the gallery above.

In the entryway to the ballroom and in the Great Hall beneath them, heads turned, eyebrows were raised, so genuine the sound of her amusement that smiles were provoked rather than frowns of censure.

Burke was not so pleased with her response. "Laugh now if you will. You were always one for laughing when it was least appropriate." There was unmasked threat in the whispered words, unmasked venom in his gaze. "You will not be laughing when I am done with you."

Blanche blinked rapidly, her fear of him palpable.

"What nonsense is this?" Melody scoffed, inwardly shaken by his tone, outwardly determined to put a brave face on it. "I have never so much as been introduced to the Earl of Erroll."

"Never been introduced? Gammon! I have it on good authority that you are to be seen everywhere in his company. In the streets of Tunbridge Wells, in church, and in his carriage gallivanting about the countryside."

A familiar burr, a heart-lifting voice gently intruded. "It is gallivanting about the ballroom I would much rather be."

Mr. Hay lounged nonchalantly in the archway behind Burke—a very changed Mr. Hay, almost a stranger. In bright red kilt and silver-clasped beaver-skin sporran, a black velvet kilt jacket, and white lace jabot. A silver crest pin held a drape of red plaid at the right shoulder, a falcon rising from a coronet.

"And who are you to so rudely interrupt our private conversation?" Burke demanded.

Most men would have quailed. Melody had seen many back down before Burke, but Dunstan smiled, this man who was given most often to sober looks. He clicked the heels of his ankle-tied Highland pumps, and doffing a red feathered Balmoral bonnet with a flourish, bowed. For a moment her gaze fixed on his bare knees—on plaid stockings bound with red flashes, at this man in what amounted to a dress. She had never seen Mr. Hay looking more handsome, fearless, or virile.

"The Earl of Erroll, sir." He said. "At your service."

Blanche was the first to respond. "The Earl of Erroll?"

"Aye. Was it not my name I heard bandied about in this most private of conversations?" His voice dropped conspiratorially. He winked at Burke. Winked at him! "Though may I be so bold, sir, as to suggest that private conversations are best conducted in private places and in a private tone of voice. Shall we adjourn to another room for those very reasons?"

"The Earl of Erroll?" Melody repeated. "You, Mr. Hay?"

"So you *are* acquainted!" Burke purred contentedly.

"Yes." She stared at Dunstan, stunned. "But . . ."

"We had no idea . . ." Blanche blurted.

"As to my title," Dunstan said apologetically. "But, aye, we are acquainted. I would go so far, sir, as to count myself among your wife's friends."

"Good friends, are you?" Burke's insinuation was snide.

"Well enough."

Snatching the document from Melody's hand, Burke slapped it against Dunstan's chest and lowered his voice. He sounded dangerous—outraged. "Well, then, sir, I've no desire to speak to you, my lord, privately or otherwise, only to share this with you, as it concerns you intimately. If you have further communications, I beg you will direct them to me by way of my solicitor."

Like one of the spotted leopard newel posts come to life, Burke slunk into the darkness from whence he came.

Chapter Thirteen

"What's this, then?" Dunstan asked, fingering the document, his gaze fixed on Melody.

Blanche, who looked more than ordinarily pale, intruded on her reply. "Is there somewhere quiet, hereabouts, my lord, where I might take a moment to catch my breath?"

"Of course!" He should have suggested as much. Both women wore rattled looks. He led them through the ballroom, a swimming throng—smiling, laughing, dancing—unaware that there were those among them in no mood for levity.

The musicians played Haydn, stately yet lilting. Too cheerful for his current mood, and yet Dunstan plastered a smile on his lips, ready with promises to return for those who would stop him. Dancers bobbed and bowed and circled on one side of them while the equally lyrical if not so mobile beauty of a marble and alabaster chimneypiece rose on the other. Carved mermaids peered down at them, dancers craned their necks to stare, at his kilt, at his company, at Lady Bainbridge unveiled.

A vicar with too broad a smile and his hand out, was circumnavigated; a heavily jeweled woman with a feathered turban whose gaze kept dropping to his bare knees turned away to whisper behind her fan. His hostess made haste to shoo her daughters out of their path, her smile never faltering. A number of young bucks fixed wolfish gazes on the lovely Lady Bainbridge. He wondered if anyone noticed, as he had, the faint bruising that still marred her complexion.

Through the doorway at the far end of the ballroom, across the landing of a smaller staircase, into the chamber that the family referred to fondly as the Withdrawing Room—withdraw, they did.

"Do you require smelling salts?" he asked Blanche.

"I do thank you for asking, but no." She sank with a sigh into a comfortable chair. "Only a moment's quiet."

Lady Bainbridge turned her back on him and crossed the cozy, tapestry-hung room to study the chimneypiece, another masterwork in a house studded with them—carved cupids riding the backs of sphinxes, each carrying a trophy of arms.

"Love conquers war," he said softly, coming up behind her, reaching out to touch one of the chubby, smiling putti.

"Tell that to the queen." Regarding him bleakly, she reached—he thought she meant to touch him—tapped instead the forgotten document he still carried. "He files a countersuit to my divorce proceedings."

"Ah!" He recovered himself enough to catch her hand before it was withdrawn, the warm silk of her flesh beneath his fingers threatening to reduce him to a mindless imbecile.

"Sorry to hear that." He stumbled over the words. "What charges?"

She withdrew her hand, cradling it to her breast like a wounded bird, before blurting, "Criminal conversation."

"Och?" Not what he had expected. Not what he wanted to hear at all. "With whom?" he asked, fearing the worst, fearing she loved another, fearing she had deceived him, as he had been deceived before.

"With you," she snapped out.

Dunstan laughed. He fairly exploded with it, relief surging from his tensed gut along with his amusement. "Me, is it?"

She frowned at him, forehead puckered.

He laughed again. Lord Bainbridge charged Lady Bainbridge with criminal conversation—the polite and legal way of accusing her of adultery—with him! It was too funny. "He shall be hard put to prove in court that which has never happened, delectable though the idea o' giving him adequate cause might be."

"Sir!" It was Blanche who objected to his forwardness. Lady Bainbridge said nothing. She had, in fact, stopped frowning at him. It was expectation he read in her gaze, not censure, and that thrilled him.

He was not to be silenced. Too elated did he feel. "Have I told you, ladies, how very bonnie you do look this evening?" He knew full well he had not, but he was not to be contained. "It is a rare treat, my lady, to see so much o' your face. Will you not bless me further with a smile?"

She flushed, frowning again. "You take this far too lightly, Mr. Hay . . . I mean, my lord Erroll . . . oh . . . I've no idea what to call you."

"You may call me whatever comes to mind," he offered expansively, his gaze flickering from the high color in her cheeks to brightened eyes, to the agitated rise and fall of her breast.

"It will be scandalous," she retorted.

"Melody!" Blanche said.

He could not stop himself from teasing. "What name would you be thinking of then?"

"Name? No! I mean this legal business. It will be both scandalous and expensive."

"Indeed!" Blanche interjected.

"I can afford it," he said, his gaze hungrily reading every emotion that passed across features he had long yearned to see.

"How fortunate for you," she said bluntly, her mouth pinched, her eyes taking on a hunted look. "I cannot afford this foolishness. My husband is now in possession of all property that once was mine. What little money from my dowry that has not already been spent on Burke's debts is now used against me in this stupid counterclaim. I already depend too much upon my uncle to pay for the solicitor's efforts on my behalf. I would not further burden him."

The money, it worried her too much, he thought. "I see," he said.

"Do you?"

"Aye. I think I do."

"Of course we do," Blanche comforted.

"I am sure Mr. Hay does not," Melody flung at her.

"I'll not argue with you, my lady." Dunstan refocused her attention. "But as it is my name your reputation is adversely connected with, I feel my purse should bear all expenses incurred."

"You cannot seriously expect me to so indebt myself to you, my lord."

"I can and do, Melody Bainbri—"

"Please!" She stopped him. "I beg you will refrain from addressing me by that hateful name." She sounded petulant, and from the way she rubbed at her temple, he guessed she suffered from the headache.

"Och, yes. I am forgetting you no longer care for it. And yet, you never did tell me what you'd rather I called you."

She blinked and backed away, the hunted look stronger. "And you? What shall I call you now, my lord? Why did you not tell us you were the Earl of Erroll?"

"I thought you knew."

"And why should you think so?"

She was hurt. He could hear the pain in her anger.

"You knew me for a falcon," he said, stroking the silver crestpin at his shoulder. "At High Rocks." He shrugged. "I thought it was your way of telling me you knew me."

"No!" She laughed at the idea. "I knew only that you reminded me of a bird of prey. It was most unkind of you not to inform us as to your true identity."

"Can you no' guess why I might hesitate?"

"I am in no mood for guesswork, sir!"

"Why did you wear a veil?" he asked her.

"You know very well why she wore that veil!" Blanche rose to her defense.

"Aye. I do know." His gaze shifted from Melody to Blanche and back again. "She wore it to hide an embarrassment, a private thing, a matter that would color people's opinion of who and what she is."

"And what has any of this to do with your not telling us you are the Earl of Erroll, Mr. Hay?"

He shrugged. "My title does, on occasion, color people's opinion of who and what I am. I wanted a veil o' sorts, myself." He fixed his gaze on Melody's stormy blue eyes. "I am guilty of wishing to know if an Englishwoman, a woman of quality, would be at all interested in who this Scotsman is. How he thinks. What matters to him—if she was no' first privy to the knowledge that he bore title, land, and money."

"You hold our sex in very low opinion, sir," Melody snapped.

"Yes. There are any number of women who would care to know you," Blanche assured him.

He sighed and turned his back on both of them. "I am not so certain. But, I am sorry to have deceived you."

"I am sorry to have allowed myself to trust a man again, to have been such a fool." Melody's voice strengthened.

"Melody, dear!"

"No, Blanche, I will have my say. I had promised myself I would never again fall prey to a man's lies, to his deceit, never again fall prey to feel—"

The door to the room opened, a sudden burst of light and sound to interrupt this passionate outpouring. Lady Sackville swept in.

To what? Dunstan wondered. To feelings? What had she meant to say?

Their hostess was bound and determined to be introduced to her unknown guests, to see to their needs, to rescue her guest of honor from the clutches of so few, that he might circulate once again among the many. Was it punch the ladies were needing? They must come, meet her friends, entertain themselves with music and dancing, not hide away in the Withdrawing Room. News had just been brought to them from London. The third vote had been taken. The Lords had failed yet again to form a majority. The king's divorce suit was to be dropped. Was it not wonderful news?

"Is it?" Blanche said unexpectedly, her gaze fixing on Melody.

"Mrs. Claybourne is feeling faint," Dunstan claimed, crossing the room with some haste to stand solicitously at Blanche's shoulder. "I wonder, have you any smelling salts, Lady Sackville?" His hand came firmly down on Blanche's shoulder? when she would protest her need for such a thing.

She jumped beneath his unexpected touch. Her contradictory "But I . . ." was stilled until Lady Sackville sailed from the room. Yes, indeed, she had smelling salts. They had only to be sent for.

As soon as the door closed behind her, Blanche voiced her objection. "I've no need of smelling salts, Mr. Hay, and well you know it."

"Aye. I know." He bent to murmur in her ear, "But, do you mind keeping Lady Sackville busy?"

"I should very much like to ask that woman why she was so heartless as to invite Lord Bainbridge to attend her entertainment!" Blanche huffed.

"Perhaps it would be more politic to inquire about the Reynolds." He waved at the portrait that graced the wall before them, his hand moving in an arc to encompass the open door at the far end of the room. Melody, her back to them, peered into its darkness. "You might even be so good as to tell her Raphael is of no interest to you."

Blanche frowned, inquiring sarcastically, "But he does interest you?"

"Indeed, he does," he admitted. "Especially if he provides a moment alone wi' your cousin."

She eyed him sharply, the frown undiminished.

He leaned closer to whisper, "You are savvy enough to see that we have much to discuss now that her husband lodges damaging charges against the two of us?"

Blanche's mouth fell open. She blinked owlishly and nodded.

"Thank you," he said, bounding away from her side, taking up a candle that he might illuminate the darkness into which Melody Bainbridge had disappeared.

She swiveled on her heel as light from his candle invaded the enormous blackness of the Cartoon Gallery, illuminating first the pale golden shine of the oak floor, then from the wall the fall of a painted red cape, the pale oval of an upturned face, the sinuous curve of a bare buttocks. She faced him, uneasy.

The pale wink of his knees in the darkness seemed unseemly provocative as he crossed to one of the deep-set windows. The flickering light threw odd shadows from the opulently carved figures guarding the window casement. Sliding back the pocket shutters, he set his candlestick upon the sill, the flame dimming the golden guinea brightness of the moon that had been tossed into the dark sky above the garden.

"Now, tell me, what were you interrupted in saying?" he suggested, his voice as gentle as always, that very gentleness troubling.

"I do not know," she lied, skirting the limits of the pale sphere of light. "Can't remember. Must not have been too important."

"Oh, but I think it was. You were saying you were sorry to have allowed yourself to trust a man again, that you had promised yourself you would not fall prey to lies and deceit and to feelings, was it?" His features were a study of light and shadow, more hawklike than ever.

"Something like that," she allowed.

"I know about such promises, such feelings." His tone changed, arresting her attention.

"Do you?" She was not convinced.

"Aye. Promised myself bachelorhood, I did, after a disappointment of the heart. Convinced myself I was happier alone, that your sex was too cruel, too clever."

"Cruel to you?"

"Aye. It is not men alone who are liars and cheats." His proud profile was a darkness edged in gold.

"Oh?" What story waited behind those few sad words, she wondered, hoping he would say more.

He was not forthcoming.

"I suppose there is truth in that," she said.

"I had promised myself I would never marry if it meant years of hard words and dissatisfaction. I vowed never to suffer heartache over any female. It is a promise I find I canna' keep."

"No?"

He turned to face her, one cheek gilded by candlelight, the other lost in shadow. "Nay. Not when I find myself so taken."

She hugged herself and backed away from him.

"Oh?" She hated that her voice trembled, despised her wayward gaze as it focused with fascination on the drape of his kilt, the nakedness of his knees. What did a man wear beneath the belted kilt, she wondered.

He turned his head, and sighed. His breath snuffed the candle. Darkness engulfed them, but for the moon.

She gasped.

Fear fingered along the nape of her neck. Had he moved from the window? His presence filled the room.

"It started with your laugh," he said.

She could not tell from whence his voice came.

"Even, without laughter, there is wit, a canny mind, a sensitive soul." His voice seemed to follow her. "How could I no' feel drawn to you, my lady?"

Eyes adjusting to the moonlight, she made some sense of the room. "You forget I am still a married woman."

"I do no' forget." Was it a trace of sadness she detected in the statement?

A clink, as if of metal. Her head swiveled to find the source.

"There is something grand between us." Another sound, as if something tore, the striking of a match. Light bloomed in front of the window, reflected in the pane, a match held to the candlewick. He had not moved, stood by the window still. "Something"—he lifted the candleholder, crossing the room to light candles in a wall sconce—"as powerful as this light in the darkness." Advancing, he lit a second sconce. "From the moment we met." Candlestick in hand, he approached her and held the light high that he might regard her expression. "Have you no sense of it? Say it is so, to my face, no veil between us, here in the light, and I will walk away, ne'er to trouble you again."

"It would be best."

The light wavered, caught in the draft of her words.

Shielding the flame, he stepped closer. "Tell me that you feel nothing for me. Eye to eye."

She could not look at him. She glared at his knees instead. "This is ridiculous."

He captured her chin in his free hand. "Eye to eye." His voice dropped. She could feel the heat of his hand on her cheek, of his breath on her mouth, of the potential of his exposed thighs, so close to hers. He lifted the candle, the better to gaze at her. Heat flared between them.

Jasper green his eyes were, shot through with gold in the changing light. Melody could not stop herself from staring. "I . . ." she began.

"Aye?"

"Feel."

"Aye?"

Her voice failed.

His brows rose. His lips parted in a sardonic smile.

She was no longer sure of the truth. No longer sure of anything, but that she did not want him to pull away.

"Do you ken how great is my need to touch you, my lady?" The hand that cupped her chin fanned out, fingertips brushing in a lingering pathway, ever so gently, across her throat, up the bone of her jaw, testing the sensitive spot just behind her earlobe. She shuddered, arching into his touch, as a cat stretches into a stroking hand.

"Yes," she whispered, afraid to look at him, unable to stop herself from doing so.

He leaned forward. The candle shook in his grip; the flame, reflected, seemed to burn in his eyes. She backed away, forcing his hand to fall, fastened her gaze on his legs again.

"Do you feel, my lady . . ." He made no attempt to pursue. " . . . there is sufficient reason for my continued restraint?"

She closed her eyes on the temptation of his lips, his arms, on the potential that sang between them, on the wonder of knowing he wanted her as much as she wanted him. Her jaw tingled with the memory of his touch. Her lips felt swollen with need.

"I would not make truth of the falsehoods with which my husband charges me."

"It is not a criminal conversation I would have wi' you," he whispered.

"Is it not?"

"Nay. Merely a polite introduction o' my lips to yours."

She inhaled deeply, tore her gaze from all contact with him, turned her back to cross to the window, and, wrapping her arms across her bosom, stared past her own reflection into the darkness. "I will admit to some feeling for you, sir. Just what that feeling may be, is not yet clear, but you expect too much, too soon, if you think I can offer more than that admission while still bound in the eyes of God and the law to another man."

The man in the moon looked back at her, distant and golden. Mr. Hay, reflection superimposed upon that moon, joined her in the glass. He positioned himself carefully, she saw—close but not touching.

"In your eyes, in your heart, are you still bound to him?" His gaze met hers by way of the window.

She shook her head.

Chapter Fourteen

Knole, November 10, 1820

The onion made him smile. Tall and topsy-turvy, marble-size bulbs perched at the top of the stalk, like fat, pearly blossoms, rather than at the bottom, where every other onion grew, its very American contrariness pleased him. The Egyptian onion it was called, though why it should be Egyptian when it came from Maine, was a mystery even the head gardener could not solve. "You must take a bunch of these with you," he claimed. "They have been a happy transplant and come from a climate very much like Scotland's."

It was not just the onion. Life pleased Dunstan. He would not deceive himself. He was content, more than content, deliriously happy, so beside himself he could not stop a stupid grin from taking complete possession of his lips even in the face of the acrid pungency of onions.

She cared for him, shared his blossoming affections, had planted in him hope and desire.

Even the muggy heat of the stove house pleased him. It seemed appropriate he should work himself into a bit of a lather in the uncommonly tropical temperatures. A large sort of lean-to built into the south face of the walled garden, glassed in on the leaning wall, it was a bright, humid place, the light filtering greenly through the creep of melon and cucumber vines and the staggered risers of potted plants, from carefully shaped orange and lemon trees, to mango, pineapple, raspberry, and strawberry plantings. A few peach trees were trained in pretty patterns along the wall.

The melon vines, encouraged to wend their way up wooden lattices in the corner, were heavily pregnant with fruit, like crazed pottery globes, richly aromatic in a place redolent with life, damp soil, and sulphur. The weighty promise of ripening, pendulous fruit, golden riches safely cradled in individual growing nets, they were a dangling breastlike femininity in the plant world. And beside them, the stiff, thrusting, yellow-tassled fulsomeness of the cucumber, their rigid green lengths both protected and magnified in thick, bell-shaped cucumber glasses. The buzz of a bee, busily pollinating, was all it took to bring to full fruition the image of a Garden of Eden here in the hothouse.

Breaking into a cheerful whistle that he was forced on occasion to abandon, for one could not simultaneously smile and whistle, Dunstan gathered a number of fine specimens.

It did not matter to him that he had been named in a libelous legal proceeding, that he stood accused by the foulest, fork-tongued snake to whom he had ever suffered the displeasure of an introduction, that even if he did not lose the case, it would cost him a great deal in money and reputation. All that mattered was that Melody Bainbridge cared for him. He wished to offer her his name along with his cucumber.

She had wanted to kiss him. He had read the inclination unerringly in her expression, in every movement of her body, in every nuance of voice and gaze. Part of him wished she had given in to her desires, that he had given in to his, that they had, both of them, given Burke Bainbridge just cause for his vengeful suit. He would take great pleasure in planting his seed in her hothouse. And yet—his smile broadened—he held her in even higher esteem that she had refrained. Tasteful restraint Lady Bainbridge exhibited, ever ladylike and refined.

He wished he might have said the same of his mother when she charged into the humid closeness of the glasshouse, throwing the stones of her displeasure. Handkerchief dabbing the immediate bloom of perspiration from her upper lip, a flurry of leafy fronds left quaking in her wake, as she approached, she fairly shouted, "I understand you have formed an attachment."

"Good day to you, mother," he began. "I had no idea . . ."

She cut him short. "Has the world gone mad? I am just arrived from London where the city celebrates the queen's victory, though there is no question she is guilty of all charges brought against her."

"As guilty as the king on those same charges?"

"Never mind the king's guilt. You certainly have no business casting aspersions when you flaunt your own partiality for a married woman in this very house! Under the nose of a duchess, no less! A cherished acquaintance, whose good opinion I would not care to lose."

"I am pleased to see that the water I sent revives your spirits, Mother." His polite tone did nothing to calm her.

"No putting me off with niceties, young man," she huffed, shaking the falcon-topped head of her cane. "Is it true what I hear? That you shamefully dangle after a married woman?"

"There is nothing shameful in my behavior, Mother. Nor do I dangle."

"But the female. She *is* married?"

"At present," he admitted tersely. "The *lady* seeks a separation."

"Lud! I feel faint!"

He caught her elbow before she could make good her words. "Come," he said. "A breath of air will revive you."

Her footsteps might seem uncertain and halting, but her tongue was not. She seemed to think nothing of how public a place for her argument was the gar-

den. "Is it to be believed that you were closeted away
with this temptress?" she said, voice rising. "For nigh
onto an hour? At a ball where you were guest of
honor? Am I to understand your hostess was forced
to winkle you away from her clutches?"

In the garden, cooler and brighter than the stove
house, the stirring of air kissed Dunstan's brow. He
studied the backs of several of the undergardeners,
bent to their tasks, and said, low-voiced, "She is no
temptress. Other than that, your spies are well informed."

"Spies!" she snapped.

"Come. We shall continue our conversation in the
pot shed." He set off without waiting to see if she followed.

"The pot shed?" Outraged, she trailed after him.
"You expect me to follow you into a pot shed?"

"Aye! There is work to do, and we shall find a bit o'
privacy."

Without another word of demur, she followed him
into the small, brick, pitch-roofed shed, though it
smelled of dirt, soil improvers, and sulphur, and she
must needs lift her skirt to avoid the damp about the
stone sink in the corner, while ducking her head to
avoid the rafters, from which tubers, bulbs, and
seeded samples had been twine-tied to dry. Like an
upside-down garden they dangled, leaves turned to
parchment, stems like sticks, roots a bristling veg-
etable hair.

Dunstan set to work clearing a stool. His mother
eyed it with disfavor, declining its meager comfort.

He shrugged, and reached high, tested the dangling
samples, pulled down those that had not a trace of
moisture, and packed the bulbs in straw-stuffed bags
or trays of sand as dry and abrasive as his mother's
voice.

"I would know, Dunstan—you must tell me—what
prompts you to behave in such a scandalous fashion?"

"Is it scandalous? Or merely the mode?"

She shooed away a fly. "Have you lost your mind to fall for such a woman?"

"Not mind, Mother, heart."

"Do not tell me you are truly smitten." She wrung her hands.

He smiled, without word or nod, and continued at his business.

"In love? This is no mere dalliance?" As persistent and wearing as the drip of water from the spigot in the stone sink, she was.

"I mean to marry her if she will have me."

"Good God! You cannot be serious!" She leaned against the stool.

"And why should I jest about such a thing?"

She sank onto the seat, letting it prop her up entirely. "But this is far worse than I ever imagined."

How quickly she returned him to childhood feelings of inadequacy. "I must admit, Mother, your sensibilities surprise me." He spoke calmly, his word choice alone evidencing his pique as he strung together his Egyptian onions. "I thought you would be thrilled I had found ground at last in which to plant the family seed."

"Thrilled? When your children by her will be bastards?"

"I have never known you to be so crass, Mother, as I find you in this instant."

She waved her hand at him, as though his insult in no way affected her. "The law is crass, not I."

"How so?"

"Was she too young to agree to the marriage?"

"Nay."

"Was he too old to consummate?"

"He beats her, Mother!" He backed into a shelf of neatly stacked pots, toppling a row.

She waited for the clatter to subside. "Is he mentally incompetent or sexually impotent? Is the marriage in any way fraudulent?"

"Noo. I've noo idea. Noo intention of asking. And noo." He put a period to each point with the noisy restacking of pots in pots. "Is it not enough that he strikes her?"

She shook her head sadly. "Well, it may be enough for a divorce *a mensa et thoro . . .*"

"From bed and board?"

"Yes, if she can prove his cruelty extreme, or that he is guilty of adultery." She rose and paced the dim aisle behind him, her reply impatient, as if he were far too slow in grasping the matter. "But, my dear boy, it is not *a vinculo matrimonii*, not freedom from the bondage of marriage."

"Meaning?" The pots were safely restored to their neat rows.

"Meaning, they will be legally separated due to his violences to her. Adultery or bestiality is equal cause."

He peeled off his gardening gloves, mulling her words. "Then this charge of his against me does nothing more than duplicate the results she has already set in motion?"

"Precisely. What is most regrettable is that in such cases the ecclesiastical court's decree is not an absolute dissolution of the bonds of marriage. Neither will be free to remarry."

The pot shed seemed suddenly too dark, too musty, too close. Head bent, footsteps leaden, Dunstan walked to the door and leaned against the jamb. The breeze kissed his temples and ruffled cool, soothing fingers through his hair. A warbler called blithely from the top of the wall, the sweetness of its song almost painful. His mother filled the doorway beside him. The bird fluttered away, a speckled flash dappled in sunlight.

"You did not know?" she asked, her voice unusually gentle.

"Nay." Smoothing hair away from his forehead, he fought to calm the galloping surge of helplessness that threatened to leave him weak-kneed. "I must admit I am not familiar with the laws governing separations. Never saw the need, as I had yet to be married, but I canna' believe my God is so unfair a deity as to desire one of His creatures to be bound to another when he would brutalize her."

She shook her head. "Well, I cannot speak for God, but as to the law, it is most unfair and doubly so for women. Men formulated these decrees, and to their own advantage."

"They do no' serve me. Not in the least." The lush green variety of the garden seemed suddenly foreign, overly voluptuous to him. He was, in many ways, so very far from Scotland.

"They will not serve Lord or Lady Bainbridge well in this case."

"It is madness!"

Her shadow nodded at his feet. "Any chance he will drink himself to death?"

"Not soon enough. More likely he will provoke someone into killing him, but on such hopes I canna' build a future."

"Can you give her up, Dunstan?"

"No!"

She sighed and pushed through the doorway, voice and manner brusque. "Do as your father did."

"My father?" He followed her. "What has he to do with any o' this?"

She bent to pluck a sprig of thyme, then pulled it apart as she walked. The herb perfumed her passage. "He kept the woman he loved."

"You knew?"

"About her?" she snapped. "Not at first. Not until I was carrying you did I discover that he loved another, that I was no more than the naive fool who provided him with an heir."

"You would encourage me to torture another innocent so cruelly? No better than Father?"

She shook her head and flapped her hands at him, dropping the thyme. Her voice was choked. "No! But neither would I have you give up too easily what I sacrificed so much to hold onto."

He fished for a handkerchief and handed it over. "The inheritance?"

"Of course the inheritance." She dabbed at her eyes.

"I see." He said it gently.

"Do you?" Rage chased away her tears.

"Yes! But it is not an heir I am after. It is the love o' my life." He turned his back on her and strode away.

She called after him, desperation thinning her tone. "I would warn you, Dunstan." Birds, more than a dozen dark fluttering shapes, exploded from the hedges. "I will turn my back on you, shut my doors to your entry, stop my ears to your every correspondence should you throw it all away." Her words, terrible in their implication, echoed from the garden walls. A dark feather drifted from the sky.

He stopped, turned, and caught the feather as it fell, smoothing it between his fingers as he eyed her gravely. With quiet conviction he responded, "I canna' throw *her* away, Mother. I will not."

Chapter Fifteen

Tunbridge Wells, November 11, 1820

That she should open the door on a day gloomy and chill with the threat of rain to the knock of Mr. Hay—whom she must now grow accustomed to thinking of as Lord Hay—that he stood hat in hand in the hallway, a tight, teasing smile upon his lips, a gentle gleam in his eyes, was an unexpected pleasure. Yet even as her heart leapt to see features grown dear, to hear the songlike burr, to read in his expression the same profound feeling of connection that bloomed in her own heart, he was telling her he meant to leave, to return to London.

"On business," he said, his voice echoing in the stairwell, chilling her more than the weather.

"Immediately?" She shivered, unwilling to believe he could so abruptly abandon her.

He nodded. "My carriage waits in the street, but there is something I would have of you before I go." His eyes burned with a hint of mischief, of affection.

As if uncomfortable with his own suggestion, he looked about, tipped his hat to someone whose footsteps sounded on the stairs below, and linked his gaze to hers again, the connection a heated one, almost feverish in its intensity. Otherwise, his every body movement was restrained. He had always been thus—a gentleman of quiet power, of studied grace, of deeply buried emotion.

What would he have of her? Idle thoughts set

checks and lips to burning. "I am very sorry I cannot invite you in, my lord, but you find me alone." *Alone, alone.* The word echoed hollowly in the stairwell.

He shifted his weight uneasily, his gaze sweeping the quiet sitting room over her shoulder. "Blanche?"

"Gone to the shops." She clung to the door, to her resolve that it must not be flung open to him.

"Ah." There burned something so warm in his regard it sparked answering fire in her veins. Gesturing the link between them with a wave of his hand, he leaned against the doorjamb and said suggestively, "Our business is pressing, do you not agree?"

She followed the movement of his hand, and then knew not where to look. He wore the appearance of a man aroused. "In what way pressing?" She piped, her voice too high, as breathless as she felt.

His smile widened. His eyes sparkled dangerously. "Do you no' feel a sense of urgency, my lady?"

"Urgency?"

"Or privation? A feeling of constraints most uncomfortable?" He leaned closer with every word.

"Constraints?" Blood burned in her cheeks, throbbed too loud in her ears. It ached in her most private parts.

"Indeed." He tapped the wood between them with his knuckles. "Of time, of title, of morality. I would cast aside society's chains."

She clutched the door tighter, then took a half step away from him.

"To do so . . ." His eyes, his mouth, his very sentence hung weighty with potential, his lips only inches from hers.

"Yes?" she breathed.

"I find myself in need of a solicitor."

"A solicitor?" she repeated stupidly. The words seemed a non sequitur.

"Aye. Perhaps a barrister as well."

He spoke of law, not lust. It was the business of Burke brought them together today, not desire. "Of course," she said, flustered, "I am so sorry. I wish—"

He caught the hand that flew out to him, his flesh to hers like flint striking steel. "No apologies, please. No wishful thinking." Pressing her fingers between his own, he carried them to his lips, his gaze hungry. "I know we are of like mind when I suggest the sooner we set to work on this charge your husband has filed, the better." He released his hold. "Do you recommend your man?"

He moved too fast for her, and never in the anticipated direction. She had yet to completely reconcile herself to the idea that he meant to go away. "Mr. Whitfield?" She cleared her throat, and tried to clear her mind. "I have little on which to judge his skill, or its absence, but I believe he is a trustworthy man. He did, on occasion, some paperwork for my father."

"Have you his direction? I should like to call on him. Even if I hire a different man, the two will surely end up in consultation."

"Of course," she agreed. "I have only to search out his card? You will wait?"

He hovered uncertainly, then backed up a step. "It would be best if I did not dally. Do you mind terribly bringing the address down to me in the street?"

"The street, my lord?" Did he suffer second thoughts about the feelings he had so recently professed to her? Nervous as a scalded cat he seemed. Shame and disappointment burned in her cheeks, ached in her heart.

"Aye." He nodded, frowning, his thoughts inscrutable. "If you will be so good."

A few moments later she went down to him, address in hand, along with a note to Whitfield indicating her desire he should assist the Earl of Erroll in all ways possible. Wrapped against the bite of the breeze in a hooded pelisse, wrapped against the bite of her own hopes in the veil of intent, she would be calm, cool, distanced. She would not wear her heart on her sleeve.

He paced the pavement in front of the boarding-house, coatless, seemingly oblivious to the chill, though little clouds of steam issued from the mouth and nose of this Scottish lord she had once believed a gardener.

How could she have been so blind? There was nothing in the least common in stance, stride, bearing, or attire. His waistcoat, sober in color and cut, his linen, immaculately pressed, pristinely white, was understated elegance. She longed to free his throat from its neckcloth prison, to ruffle the smooth sweep of tawny brown hair, to expose the heated passion that hid beneath his collected thoughtfulness.

"Are you not cold, sir?" she asked, her own body tensed against the chill, against the impending loss of him.

"Nay, not cold," he said quietly, breath pluming. "It is overheated I am."

Her breath froze in her throat.

His look was meant to melt her. "You are no' an unschooled virgin, my lady. Do not play the part of one. Surely you ken I burn with desire."

She feared her feelings would make her foolish. "Desire to be gone, sir?" she blurted, knowing full well that was not at all his meaning.

He shook his head. "To the contrary. But perhaps your passion has cooled along with the weather?"

He confused her. Her own feelings confused her. She wanted to stay him, but feared admitting as much. Clenching teeth against the cold and knees against the heat of her need, she handed him Mr. Whitfield's address. "I have no desire to delay your departure, sir." It was a bold-faced lie.

He took the slip of paper, made a show of unfolding it, of reading it, and yet his words, when he spoke, had nothing to do with Whitfield. "What *have* you desires for, my Lady Bainbridge?"

You! She longed to shout, saying instead, "I have every desire to be quit of the bane that bridges my identity, of the ridiculous charges with which my husband plagues me, of the fear—"

"Fear?"

"That he will manage in some manner to keep me bound to him."

"Nothing more?" His jasper green eyes spoke as much of disappointment as did his voice.

Of course she desired more. She wanted word or look or gesture from him with which to confirm her own feelings of wonder, of desire, of a love too amazing to relinquish or ignore—some sign that his heart was touched, even bound to her. She wanted promises. She wanted hope. She could not bear to lose the dream of him, the potential. She had only just discovered Dunstan Hay and how much he meant to her. But she dared not voice her neediness. His coach stood waiting to whisk him away from her, perhaps forever. She hated the sight of it.

"Across the street," he murmured.

The roan! Hip-shot, head low, it stood patiently, swinging its tail, switching flies at one of the hitching rings in front of the inn. But it was not the horse Dunstan Hay would have her observe.

"Do ya' see the fellow blowing a cloud?"

A man, squat and portly, lounged in the shadowed inset doorway to the inn, one hand plunged in his pocket, the other, mittened, rolling a cigar between his lips, plucked free on occasion for the exhalation of smoke.

"I see him."

"Ha' you seen him before?"

"I do not think so. He is not the sort of fellow to capture my attention."

"My guess, he has been hired by your husband to keep you under observation."

She did her best to hide the fear that nibbled the nape of her neck. "Dear me. What a boring job for the man." She tried to laugh and failed. No laughing matter if this was the same roan she had seen at High Rocks and from the window at Penshurst Hall.

Dunstan's expression sobered. "He would be particularly interested in any interaction between you and me."

"Undoubtedly." She laughed again—did a better job of it.

Mischief returned. "Thank heaven he was no' invited to the duchess's ball."

"But nothing happened."

"Nothing?"

Heat bloomed in her cheeks. "Nothing that might be used against us in court."

"Then you will admit something happened?"

"Yes." She shivered with an intensity of feeling. "Indeed. Something happened."

"Shall we give the little man something to report? I am yearning for a kiss good-bye," he whispered huskily. "Nay, now, no laughing. Our nosey observer will report we enjoy ourselves far more than is fitting."

She could not subdue her amusement, smiling wryly at the carriage wheels rather than face him. "I had no idea you were given to self-destructive tendencies, my lord."

"Not self-destructive, self-indulgent. You must teach me restraint." He reached for the door handle.

She stayed his hand. "Can it be done, Mr. Hay?"

His left brow rose provocatively. "I am a swift learner, sufficiently motivated."

She shook her head and bit back a laugh. "You mistake my meaning. Can a solicitor prove our innocence?"

"We must hope so, or both our lives and any hope for future happiness are ruined, my lady."

He called her "my lady," as was his habit, and yet such was his pronunciation of those three syllables that she realized he did in fact say her name— Melody—that he had been referring to her as such for quite some time.

"You say my name," she said.

His smile, imp of mischief that it was, returned. "Aye. Will you no' make me the happiest of men in returning the intimacy, my lady Melody?"

Milady, Melody. The words chuckled from his tongue like water playing over pebbles.

She managed a laugh. "I shall miss your teasing manner, my lord." No longer did she duck his gaze, guard her desire, or hide in laughter. "May we meet again soon, Dunstan," she said earnestly.

His smile broadened. His gaze was a visual caress. "Indeed! There is a matter of some importance I would discuss with you as soon as this knotty business with your husband is unraveled."

She lost herself in the love in his eyes. "There is much I would discuss with you, too, sir, were I but free."

"Freedom. Yes." His brows knit. It was with a thoughtful expression he climbed into the carriage and pulled the door shut, leaning through the open window to briefly clasp her hand, saying, "I mean to work on that."

She watched the carriage pull away, watched the man across the street as he, in turn, watched her, troubled by a sudden fear of what harm might come to her in Lord Hay's absence.

A passing chaise blocked the view of her most immediate concern. She turned to enter the boarding-house, but was stopped by the sounds of a carriage stopping, overriden by a man's voice calling the name she despised. "Lady Bainbridge!"

She thought at first that the man with the cigar dared approach. It was not he who called, however, but a liveried footman who stepped down, hat in hand, from a crested traveling coach drawn by matched bays. A woman with a proud, forbidding countenance leaned from the window, stern features richly surrounded by an ostentatious mulberry satin bonnet with matching ribbons and feathers, the whole of which perched atop a lace-encrusted mobcap, as befit a woman of advancing years.

"A word, if you will, Lady Bainbridge." The footman gestured her forward.

Confused and curious, Melody approached the

woman. "Are we acquainted?" she asked even as the crest on the coach door, a falcon rising from a coronet, clarified to some degree who the woman was.

"By way of my son." The woman's voice was chill, unbending, and proud. Imperious in volume and tone, it leapt from her lips like the overbearing bark of a small dog. Her bonnet brim inclined in the direction Lord Hay's carriage had taken.

"Lady Hay?"

The mulberry bonnet tipped once, feathers whipping in the wind, far more animated than the woman's features.

"You have just missed your son. He is on his way to London. You may catch him if—"

"It is you I would speak to, Lady Bainbridge." Lady Hay enunciated each word with profound deliberation, her expression peeved, as if her objective were as plain as the nose down which she peered.

Melody's stomach did a turn. "Ah! You have heard of the suit with which my husband would dishonor your son?"

"I have heard a great deal of late in connection with the name of Bainbridge." Lady Hay's nostrils quivered, as if assailed by noxious odors.

"Have you?"

"Indeed I have, Lady Bainbridge." The feathers bobbed in concert with the woman's several chins. "And while we have never been introduced, I hope you will not refuse me an interview."

With a gesture to the footman, the door was thrown open, as if it were a given Melody must obey such a summons, despite the woman's dislike of her, as chill and discouraging as the day.

Outwardly, Melody strove to remain calm. Inwardly, she quaked. Of all the women in the world who might take her in dislike, who might judge her in any way unworthy, she was loath it should be this one. Through the far window of the carriage, Melody could see a fog of cigar smoke. The man stepped away from the shadows guarding the doorway to the inn. He wore a battered brown cap, the brim guarding his eyes as he sucked and rolled and blew smoke from the cheroot between bewhiskered lips. Yet beneath the cap's brim she could see he examined the crested carriage. He did, in fact, jam cigar between his teeth, pull forth a notebook, and scribble with a pencil stub he licked with almost as much relish as his cigar.

She was caught between two dragons, and only a matter of deciding if she preferred to be flambéed or fricasseed.

"I should be pleased to talk to you, Lady Hay," she said. "Your son has been very kind, at a time in my life when I was most in need of kindness."

Lady Hay waved a hand, fretting, "Get in, girl. Get in. You make me cold, standing there with the door open."

Not so much as a note left for Blanche, Melody stepped up and into the belly of the coach, swallowed up by the overpowering presence of Dunstan's mother, the dowager Lady Hay, an intimidating woman with an intimidating stare, who gave her a most searching perusal by way of her gold-rimmed lorgnette, and who refused to speak of anything substantial outside of the unfortunate turn in the weather, the prospects to be seen from fog-sweated carriage windows, or the efficacious effects to be had from the local baths.

She did mention Dunstan once, suggesting, "It was timely of my son to send north his wagon full of seedlings this morning. He will have little to keep him so far south, now that his business is concluded."

"Indeed." She could think to say no more.

"Yes." Lady Hay seemed displeased to provoke so little response. "Very inconvenient that this business should drag him back to London, when it is quite the opposite direction he would most like to be headed. He will want to be in Scotland soon, to attend to the delivery and disposition of so many perishables."

Melody found the woman's insistent suggestion that Dunstan Hay had much better things to do insulting. "Will he?" she asked mildly. "Has he not servants to tend to such detail?"

"Of course." Lady Hay drew back as if she had been slapped. Eyes narrowed, she tried a different tack. "You will admit it is most annoying—this trip to London?"

"A vicious character assassination and unnecessary legal proceedings, I would agree, can be most annoying."

Lady Hay smiled and nodded, but there was no real sense of agreement in her eyes as she looked at and through Melody, rapping briskly on the coachman's trap to bark, "You will turn here!"

The requested turn carried them with a rude jolt off the well-paved London road onto one of the dirt tracks that struck a brown stripe northwesterly across the wide, empty solitude of the common green.

"Where do you take me?" Melody asked.

"Where do *I* take *you*, Lady Bainbridge?" Lady Hay's emphasis leant the words fresh and unintended significance. "We are going nowhere." Her mouth was slammed shut involuntarily as they hit a particularly deep rut in a crossroad that led, if the sign was to be believed, to a gravel quarry. "The trees," she called harshly to the driver.

A grove loomed ahead of them, oak, beech, and poplar alive with color: flame red, burnt orange, old gold. In the bright, crisp weather one could see things for miles with great clarity. Melody began to think Lady Hay equally transparent.

In a flurry of skittish leaves, the coach was drawn to a halt, the door opened, and the ladies handed out. The footman, who would follow them, was turned back with an impatient gesture.

Lady Hay murmured, "Yes. This will do nicely. A bit of privacy is to be had here."

They were surrounded by an unpeopled landscape.

Melody laughed and spread her arms. "An abundance of privacy, Lady Hay."

Lady Hay was not amused. She did, in fact, scowl quite forbiddingly.

To prevent a second outburst of unwelcome laughter, Melody went on as seriously as she could. "Of what would you speak to me that requires so much of that commodity?"

"You know very well of what and whom I would speak to you. All of Tunbridge Wells speaks of it, and most of London."

Humor quelled by such rudeness, Melody feigned ignorance. "Is it the king's case against his queen, you mean? I understand all of London celebrates the queen's victory."

"Small victory, that. Do not exasperate me with mindless babble, girl. You must know it is your separation, your proposed divorce, interests me far more than the king's failed one."

Melody lifted her face to the trees, a rustling flutter of butterscotch and wine drifting from a cerulean heaven. The edge to the breeze, the smell of damp earth, of decaying leaves, filled her head with the strongest sense of change. There was something sad in the season, in the approach of winter, something exhilarating, too. The trees undressed themselves, that they might regarb in fresh foliage with the coming of spring.

With a sense of sadness, of failure, of endings, she asked, "Why does my private disappointment so interest you?"

"Because your private disappointment, as you would so style it"—Lady Hay flung the words at her—"directly affects Dunstan. You will ruin him, you know." Her voice was flat, hard, her gaze locked, scowling, on the horizon. A solitary rider threatened their privacy.

Melody floundered, caught off guard. "But there is no truth to my husband's charges."

"Charges? Never mind the charges." Lady Hay plucked free a golden leaf from its tenuous hold to a branch that reached between them, tossing it aside without pause to marvel at its beauty. "It would be best if you removed *yourself* from his company."

The truth was painful. "Best for whom?" Melody snapped, knowing full well the answer, knowing, and hating the knowledge.

Lady Hay barked a rueful laugh. "Best for Dunstan, of course. I believe, in truth, you love my son. You would be in a position to recognize a worthwhile gentleman, now that you have been shackled for some time to something less. I hope you do love him. My task is easier if you care for my son. If you love him, you will do what is best. Union with a woman who can bear him nothing but bastards cannot be the best life has to offer Dunstan."

Melody's mind whirled, as wind-tossed as the leaves. How did one respond to a reality one wished untrue?

Lady Hay expected no response. She shook her head emphatically, feathers dancing, her every word barbed. "A life without hope of passing his name, or the wealth and land he has been so careful to foster, the monies he has so carefully invested—none of it to go to his children, or his children's children. Do not tell me you think that can be good for him. I will not believe a word of it if you do."

Defenses crumbling, heart pierced by hard truths she had long denied, Melody said sharply, "Do you imagine you can bully me away from him if I do not agree with such an assessment? If he does not?"

"Bully you?" Lady Hay laughed. "Not at all. I would, indeed, make it easier for you if you will let me. I can see you are a very strong young woman. To have done what you have done takes great fortitude, remarkable courage—more than most women can find within themselves. And yet, you will be left penniless, will you not? Without land, title, or connection? I imagine you are already an outcast among those you once called friend."

"Do you think to make it in any way easier for me,

Lady Hay, by cruelly recounting all that I stand to lose?"

"By no means. I would reveal to you what you stand to gain. I am a woman of means. I can make every mile you place between yourself and my son of value. I hear Spain is lovely at this time of year."

Chapter Sixteen

"She dared warn you away from him?" Blanche asked, highly indignant, as she and Melody walked the pathway toward the long, low building where Tunbridge ware was constructed. Blanche must have a tea caddy, perhaps a tray as well. "Whatever do you mean to do?" she asked.

The doorway to the factory yawned before them like the future, a dark portal strange with the odors of fresh-cut cedar, oak, and yew, the dizzying reek of paint, glue, stain, and finish. They were met with a flurry of pale sawdust, swallowed up in a rich, almost wincing weight of noise as they stepped into a world busy with saws, drills, the staccato rhythm of hammers, the steady rasp of sanding blocks. Sawdust, like snow, suspended in the air, powdered the hair and shoulders of the craftsmen as they worked, and drifted under foot and skirt hems in soft, aromatic piles, from palest ash to darkest ebony.

"Do?" Melody repeated faintly, feeling no more substantial than the drifts of waste wood. "I haven't the slightest idea."

They were welcomed with smiles, with nods, with a brief pause in the rhythm and noise of industry. A lad of no more than eight, whose job it would seem was the unending task of fetching, carrying, sweeping up, and carting away wood scraps, greeted them with a wide, gap-toothed grin, and said, "Show you about, ladies, should you care to be guided."

Blanche produced a coin, endearing herself to the lad, and follow they did.

"What are your options?" Blanche asked.

The lad thought the question addressed to him.

"One hundred and more woods. All different kinds and colors to choose from, ladies." With the ease of a professional cabinetmaker he pointed out the red browns of cherry, rosewood, paduak, and "horse-flesh" mahogany, the creamy yellow of ash, holly, boxwood, and yew, the patterned oddities of zebrawood, satinwood, and whorled birds-eye maple.

What were her options? Should she leave Dunstan Hay to a brighter future, as his mother suggested? Would it be kinder? She had so little to bring to a marriage, so little to offer the Earl of Erroll.

"One must choose carefully when it comes to the building materials that go into anything worthwhile," the lad suggested.

Melody flushed, shamed, as if God spoke to her through the mouth of a boy. She had not chosen carefully. For the future, in choosing the shape and substance of her tomorrows, she must be at least as careful as these craftsmen who cut and shaped wood, adze and saw fashioning beautifully intricate patterns and complex panoramas: landscapes, seascapes, still lifes—flowers, grapevines, leaves, and shells, some in mosaic bands carefully inlaid with the aid of tweezers and a steady hand, others exquisitely cut and fit together like Chinese puzzle pieces. Her life, her future, her choices ought to be arranged with just such meticulous care.

"She offered me money to go away. To Spain."

"Did she really?" Blanche gasped. "Was it very much money?"

"I've no idea." Melody laughed. "I never asked."

"No. Well, of course you did not."

They paused to observe a row of assemblers who hammered and glued together boxes, adding hinges to the carefully fitted lids, keying locks.

What is the key? Melody wondered. What key unlocked the strangely confining box her life had become?

"I hesitate to ask, my dear." Blanche jerked her away from ruminations.

"What, cousin?"

"Has the earl announced his intentions, Melody? That you would refuse outright this offer of money. You are in need of money."

"I am. And a burden to you," Melody said.

"Not at all, my dear. But you are accustomed to living well. I have not much in the way of creature comforts to offer you." She lowered her voice to a whisper. "It only seemed prudent to ask if Lord Hay offers you any permanence in his affections, in his intentions."

Melody was at a loss for an answer. That Dunstan's intentions, that the matter of which he meant to speak to her should be anything but honorable and permanent had never crossed her mind. The very suggestion that she might be fooled again by a man whom she had grown to trust angered her. She set off into a second room thick with the smell of finish. It set her eyes to watering.

Was it so inconceivable that a gentleman might offer for her once she was separated from Burke? She had shoved to the back of her consciousness the knowledge that her children would be considered bastards. Now the words, as spoken by Lady Hay, sounded like a death knell.

Two gentlemen, kerchiefs drawn over their noses, finishing rags in their hands, glanced up. Shellac stiffened their leather gloves, aprons, and shoes, stickied the floor about their feet. They were coated almost as completely in the glossy finish they wielded as the boxes they set to dry in gleaming rows.

Blanche, a lace hankie pressed to her nose, suggested, "Would that we could put such a fine, unblemished finish on our lives."

"On our hearts," Melody said softly.

Blanche cradled her new tea caddy in her hands. Constructed of the yellow sapwood of the yew, its lid was detailed with a particularly beautiful woodland panorama, a deer in the center, head raised, neck arched, surrounded by an intricate border of oak leaves in reddish orange heartwood. "It reminds me of the day we spent at Penshurst Place," she said. "Do you remember? The day we fed the deer?"

Melody looked up from the drawer she emptied. "I remember," she said quietly. Too well she remembered.

"Lord Hay—we did not know him yet as a lord— was so kind."

Melody closed her eyes, bit back a sharp retort, and said gently, "You will want to pack it in something soft."

"Something soft, yes. Would not want it to be damaged." Blanche crossed the room and hovered uncertainly at Melody's elbow.

"Here, perhaps this will do," Melody handed her a shawl.

"This sudden quitting of the Wells, Melody. I thought you made of sterner stuff than to meekly follow his mother's direction."

Melody stuffed down the anger that rose within her as vigorously as she stuffed the contents of the drawer into a carpetbag. "I do not go because she tells me to. I do not do it for her at all."

"Why then?"

All the fight went out of her in an instant. She sank onto the clothing-strewn bed.

"For him," she said flatly, her voice breaking.

"Love him, do you?" Blanche's voice was too gentle, too kind, too full of understanding.

It was no use. She could not stop the tears. A sob tore at her throat. She turned into Blanche's waiting arms. "Yes. Oh, Blanche!" The words exploded wetly against Blanche's shoulder. "God help me. I do."

Chapter Seventeen

London, November 13, 1820

With the feeling that he was moving in the wrong direction, Dunstan sped into London late in the day, horses fretting to the unexpected tune of fire-crackers popping, booming, spilling a fine shower of sparks into the darkness. Unexpected too, the light to be seen on many a street corner, bonfires that leapt and whirled along with the mobs that sang and danced around them, drunken voices and bottles raised to the tune of many a pipe whistle, fiddle, or wheezing street organ.

Dunstan passed amid the press of people—alone, no real reason for celebration. His life had taken an uncertain and nasty turn. There was an ill-humored irony, a wrenching sort of self-sabotage in always losing his heart to unattainable women. Gillian, his first love, had given herself to another. Melody Bainbridge might never be free to wear any ring, any name for that matter, but the Bainbridge she hated.

The coachman slowed the horses to a walk. At no faster pace could they push safely through the crowds, though Swan took to dark side streets and alleyways on occasion, avoiding the drunken revelers, who insisted Dunstan lower his window at every opportunity and echo the sentiment when they bellowed, "Long live the queen!"

"What's all this then?" Dunstan called when the coach was brought to yet another standstill alongside a narrow creep that ran between two buildings.

As if the question were addressed to him, a ruddy-faced gent taking a steaming piss just inside the creep, responded drunkenly, "The queen, sir, may God and Pergami savor her, is still the queen!" Belching, he lifted a rum jug in a one-handed salute, finished his watering of the cobblestones, and with a rocky-stanced shake, fumbled himself decent to cry, "Our king, may Heaven and his many angels of the night help him"—he raised his jug to his lips—"shall not have his disgraceful divorce"—a belch—"no matter how much he doth pray, pain, or penalize the Lords for it." He guffawed at his own witticism, slapped his thigh, and sank to his knees for another slug from the jug. Given his condition, Dunstan thought his remark evidenced a certain greatness of mind.

"But that was determined three days since, was it not?" Dunstan called out to him. "We heard the final vote in Tunbridge Wells."

"Better to have been in Lunnun, lad—celebrating." From the kneeling position, he raised his jug in salute, the move knocking him off balance. He swayed as he boasted. "I should be much surprised if there is a soul left in all of the city still sober." With this alliterative feat complete, he upended his jug, sighed with satisfaction when the last drop was drained, and pitched face first into his own puddle.

Dunstan woke to the sound of rain, a rain that doused the celebratory bonfires, creating sodden piles of charred chairs and broken boxes—Caroline's triumph pissed upon by the heavens. Bleary-eyed and woolen-mouthed, the revelers went back to work. London, like a wayward woman after a romping good night's business, lethargically bestirred herself.

Dunstan stared from his window at wet, fog-shrouded streets, at dripping costermongers setting up their barrows in the nearby market. It was a bleak prospect in the half-light of morning. He longed for wild, green open spaces, for a backdrop of mountains blueing the horizon. The Thames seemed an ugly, snakish, flat thing broken by nothing more than the craft who rode its back.

From the tallest masthead on the river dangled an apparition, a drenched mass of stuffed muslin, flapping canvas, and paint dampened to the dripping point.

"What is that thing, Potsby?" he asked of the gentleman who had waited on him as a boy, who waited on him still whenever he returned to his mother's house.

Potsby put down the tray he carried to peer at the "thing" in question. "That, my lord, is a twenty-five-foot bishop, hung by his heels."

"A bishop?"

"Yes, my lord. There are those who are not happy with the decision, sir, to exclude the new queen's name from the liturgy for our recently deceased monarch, to bar her from the new king's coronation."

"Has the whole country gone mad?"

"The Queenites are mad for the queen, my lord."

"And so, they dance in the streets and drink themselves stupid, and for what? That the king could not divorce her?"

"There are many who are dead set against the idea of divorce, my lord. Let no man tear asunder that which God has bound together."

"No matter how dreadful the match?" Dunstan shook his head, anger rising. "Is it truly God's will that any woman remain bound to a husband who holds her in utter contempt? Who dishonors her at every opportunity? Who has never evidenced an iota of affection for her? The queen can have no reasons to remain in such a union other than those inspired by pride, greed, and vengefulness."

"And fear, sir. Who would she be, my lord, if not the queen? What would she do—cast off, disgraced, a queen without a crown or country?"

Dunstan thought of Melody, similar of dilemma—far braver than the queen. "In my opinion Potsby, it is disgrace to which Caroline of Brunswick clings. There must be something more to the woman than crown and husband."

The bishop flapped wetly in the breeze, and Potsby, if he had an opinion, held tongue on it.

From Mr. Whitfield's office window, in Lincoln's Inn Fields, Dunstan stood staring from fresh perspective at the same sodden effigy.

"An untimely thing, these divorce proceedings," Whitfield murmured, his nose rising from the papers he perused, from which he extricated a beribboned sheaf. "Here are the marriage settlements you asked to see. Though what good they will do you I've no idea. They certainly did Lady Bainbridge no good."

The search for said documents had taken the better part of half an hour.

Dunstan turned his back on the dripping bishop, took the papers in hand, and turned to the window again the better to read them. He was not impressed with the inefficient and disorganized Mr. Whitfield, whose office was no warmer than the streets. The solicitor looked like nothing so much as a mole forced to abandon the dark comfort of its hole, hunched over a mountain of paperwork, peering through rodential spectacles, a muffler wrapped about his throat, documents clutched in fingerless woolen mitts.

Dunstan's title had stirred the man into largely ineffectual, unctuously hand-wringing motion. His request to view the Bainbridge marriage settlements had been met with a frenzied rearrangement of teetering piles of paper. Brought to light at last, Dunstan's hands shook a little in holding such solid, pen-and-ink proof of the marriage he would rather had never existed.

The carefully couched language, the official seal, the list of settlements: pin money, a jointure, a property in Surrey, portions to be settled upon potential offspring, spoke too officially of promises, of hopes, of the reality of two people binding names, title, rank, properties, and money—of two people who had sworn before God and their fellow man to love, honor and obey.

Whitfield waxed eloquent, bent on pointing out the blindingly obvious. "The country, and certainly the Lords, have no patience at the moment for more talk of divorce, you know. It is for that reason I have so long delayed Lady Bainbridge's business."

"Is it now?" Dunstan said, distracted, the page blurring before his eyes—muddied by the thought of a hopeful Melody Bainbridge making plans for her future, for a family, with the man she had taken as husband till death did they part, the man who beat her. "You have heard of the countersuit Lord Bainbridge means to file against me?" he asked quietly.

Whitfield nodded, steepled his mittened fingers, and stared over the bridge of his spectacles. "Criminal conversation, is it not? Are you in need of professional services, my lord?" He asked the question suggestively, with an annoying hint of superiority, his smile overripe.

"I would understand first what you have done to facilitate the settlement of Lady Bainbridge's original suit."

The smile soured. The steepled fingers tapped uneasily. The man's gaze refused to meet Dunstan's directly, sidling, instead, crablike, uneasy.

"Are you satisfied, sir, that it best suits your client to pursue the matter of Lady Bainbridge's abuse at the hands of her husband, rather than the possibility of some fraud he may have perpetrated against her in the marriage?"

Whitfield puffed out his chest like a challenged cockerel. "Would you place a higher priority in the possibility of fraud than in the brutal acts of which Lord Bainbridge is accused?"

"Nay. I would not, but the law does."

"You are trained, then, sir, in matters of the law? Am I to understand you are not satisfied with the job I am doing?" Whitfield's shoulders rode high. His arms folded forbiddingly across his meager chest. A muscle ticked uncontrollably in his jaw. "I suppose I should be mightily grateful that it is Lady Bainbridge hires me and not you, if such is the case."

Shrugging, Dunstan consigned the documents to the oblivion of Whitfield's nonexistent filing system. The man was a blathering idiot. Dunstan longed to wring his neck, to declare him completely incompetent, but there seemed no sign of fraudulent intent in connection with the marriage settlements. It was hope of fraud that forced Dunstan to face the pain of so much unpleasant ink on so many damnably official documents.

Disappointed he leaned forward and asked on a whim, "Are you a married man, sir? Have you ever been in love?"

"I do not see what that has to do—"

"Och, do you not! I came to you, sir, as a man in need o' sound legal counsel. I would judge, you see, if we are men of' like mind."

The cockerel made clucking noises. "I am sure, my lord, I should be happy to accommodate—"

He cut the fool short, ready to be gone. "Can matters be settled out o' court, do you think? Is Lord Bainbridge a man to be negotiated with?"

Whitfield shrugged. "One must have something with which to negotiate."

"Is scandal not enough to dissuade him? The ruination of reputation?"

"I have sent correspondence to his solicitors with that in mind. There has been no reply."

Was the man completely spineless? Why did he not insist upon a reply? Dunstan rose, afraid his contempt might too clearly be read if he continued to face the fool. "Anything else that might tempt him to settle?"

The molelike eyes brightened, the dirt-digging nose rose, as if to test the wind. "He is in need of money."

"Is he? But I had heard he is in possession of his wife's dowry."

"What little is left of it. My Lord Bainbridge is in the unfortunate habit of living above his means."

"There is mention, too, in the settlements, of a property in Surrey?"

"Ah, yes. Bainbridge Hall. Long since sold. Within months of the marriage if memory serves."

Blanche's voice rose from the bog of memory, a reference to the staircase at Bainbridge Hall. Dunstan frowned. Perhaps it was nothing. "Can you find out for me exactly when it was sold?" he asked.

It was on the same day he visited Mr. Whitfield that Dunstan first sought an exchange with Lord Bainbridge. To his lordship's apartments he went, to an ostentatiously brass-knockered door, opened by his lordship's man, a pinched-looking fellow with graying hair and the worried look of a hound dog accustomed to dodging boot toes.

"My lord is out," he said. "Do you care to leave your card?"

Dunstan did not care to leave a card he knew would provoke nothing more than outrage or contempt. He returned the following day with the same question. "Is your master in?"

Received the same response.

On the third day the man who opened the door, and it was always the same pinched old man, rolled his eyes at sight of him. Before Dunstan could so much as open his mouth, he said impatiently, as if addressing an idiot, "My lord is not in London, sir. Gone into Kent, he has. And not expected to return anytime soon. You waste your time in coming daily to ask after him. If it is payments due makes you so persistent, I will be happy to take your card and inform his lordship immediately upon his return."

"Payments? You think me a bill collector, do you?"

"Is it not money you are after?" The gentleman's eyebrows rose to a pinch above his pinched nose.

"Nay."

"What business then? If you do not mind my asking."

"On Lady Bainbridge's behalf I do call upon his lordship."

"My lady?" The old gent's voice betrayed his surprise, indeed his pleasure at mention of his mistress. "How does my lady?"

Dunstan eyed him warily. "Her bruises have faded almost entirely," he said. "Her face, you will be happy to hear, bears no permanent scar. I regret I canna' say the same for her sensibilities."

The pinched mouth pinched tighter still. "A shame, that," he said, his voice low.

"Indeed!"

"I must say I was surprised she ever returned—attempting a reconciliation. I believe that foolish cousin of hers convinced her it was a rational idea. I should have tried harder to dissuade her from stepping foot across the threshold. Did try to stop him from hitting her, you know."

"Nay. I did not know."

"Knocked me out, he did. In a black mood he was."

"So it would seem. Why do you no' leave his service?"

"More difficult than you'd think."

"How so?"

"He would, of course, refuse to recommend me to anyone."

"And Lady Bainbridge? Would she recommend you?"

He smiled. "Of course she would. But who has she left to recommend me to? Most of her acquaintances have fallen off now that she has lost money, rank, and the status of the married state. There are more than a few who consider her claims so extraordinary as to be lies. And the recommendation of a liar is no recommendation at all, now is it, my lord?"

"I see."

"Will you tell her I asked after her? That I wish her every happiness? Name's Tibalt. She'll remember me."

"I will, Mr. Tibalt."

"Would you be the Earl of Erroll, then?"

"You have heard of me?"

"Yes. My master speaks ill of you on a fairly regular basis. Pleased to meet you. The dear girl is deserving of a bit of happiness. We were all of us pleased to learn she had worked up courage to file for a separation. Even more heartened to learn she had found herself a champion."

"Is she in need of a champion, then?"

"Surely, you would know that better than anyone, my lord. He is still after her, is he not? Still bent on bending her to his will."

"And if she dinna' bend?"

"Why, sir, he will break her. He will."

Chapter Eighteen

London, November 20, 1820

Melody sat stiffly at the window, miserable, staring at the passing rain-drenched streets. *He* was in London. *He* had been to speak to Mr. Whitfield, in whose hired carriage she sat. *He* was in London and she was in London, and she dared not catch so much as a glimpse of him or all her resolve was flown. She wished him back in Scotland, happily planting cherry trees, wished him gone forever so she could stop thinking of him, stop wondering what it was he would have said to her, given the chance, stop aching and yearning and losing sleep over an unattainable future.

"Here we are!" Whitfield said brightly, throwing open the carriage door. "You come home, Lady Bainbridge!"

Melody sighed. "Not home," she said firmly. Flexing her fingers she took his hand. His grip strangled. She scowled up at the rain-drenched facade of her husband's town house. "This place never did feel like home."

It was decidedly odd, returning to the doorway she had sworn never to darken again, odd that it should be opened by Jasper Tibalt, who had once served her so faithfully, who had, in fact, suffered a broken wrist for daring to step between her and Burke in the heat of one of Burke's rages.

"Mistress!" His voice betrayed his alarm. "Whatever do you do here?"

Mr. Whitfield removed his rain-studded hat and handed Tibalt his card. "You will announce us, please. We are expected."

"As you say." He paused, as if to offer her opportunity to change her mind. "Your friend, marm, Lord Hay, has been to call."

"Has he?" She tried to evidence neither concern nor enthusiasm as she slipped off damp gloves and was helped from her wet cloak. "Did my husband receive him?"

"No, my lady. The master has only just returned from the country."

"Ah." She removed her hat and shook away the wet, forgetting for a moment that Tibalt was there to see to such things for her. "Well"—she smoothed her bodice, fingered a curl or two into place, and straightened her shoulders—"best not keep him waiting."

It was not Burke, but they who were kept waiting in the red drawing room, a room charged with past anger, a room that resounded of pain—a room changed, as if Burke would obliterate all trace of her ever having had a part in the place.

A bird dog, more at home than she, lay snoozing by the fire. A silky, long-legged water spaniel, exquisitely dappled, caramel and cream—it raised an eyebrow when they entered and lay watching them with a worried look, brow furrowed, tail thumping an uncertain tattoo. She held out her hand, would have knelt to scratch its ears had it given any friendly indication. It raised its head, but seemed otherwise disinterested. She did not insist it accept the hand of a stranger. She walked the room instead, rediscovering the place she had fled.

The French floral window hangings she had suggested had been replaced with more crimson. One could not look anywhere in the room without seeing red. Her mother's Staffordshire shepherdess figurines no longer lined the mantel. The landscapes that had once adorned the crimson damask walls had been supplanted by hunting scenes: a hawking party, the feathered spoils of the hunt piled limply in the grass, a rabbit harried by greyhounds, a still life of dead game. *Disturbing*. Melody did not care to see a glossy feathered blackcock, two pheasants, a brace of partridge, and a hare—their heads assuming an unnatural repose—deftly rendered, faithful in their lifelessness, stilled forever on the bloodred wall.

Like a strange sort of still life, themselves, they waited: she, Whitfield, and the dog she had ample opportunity to befriend. Three-quarters of an hour they waited, her hands, her nerves calmed by the dog's trusting head in her lap, his supple ears silken between her fingers. The Limoges clock on the mantel chimed thrice. Mr. Whitfield grew more impatient by the moment, consulting his pocket watch frequently, as if the clock were not to be trusted. When at long last the doors opened with a soft click, the noise seemed preternaturally loud, shocking, in the expectant stillness.

Burke strolled casually into the room, as always spare, trim, neat as a pin. He brought with him a turbulence of spirit. It eddied like a storm about him, stirring the air, affecting the attitude, the posture of all he surprised within the confines of his drawing room. To Melody it was as if a Spanish fighting bull trotted gracefully into their presence.

The spaniel stiffened and lifted its head from Melody's lap.

"Zeus! Come!" Burke addressed the animal sharply, nose high, testing the wind for impending confrontation.

Guiltily, the animal slunk, slope-shouldered toward his master, tail low, a desperately wagged white flag.

"Out!" Burke snapped his fingers and pointed toward the door.

The dog obeyed, but not without leaving behind a pale, yellow puddle.

Melody held her breath. Just the thing to set Burke off.

Burke surprised her, stepping over the urine as if it were not there.

Through the door without summons, Tibalt scuttled, mop in hand, wielding this tool with such dexterous speed he had erased the problem and quietly made exit before his master had crossed the room and settled himself in a chair.

The seat Burke chose was to Melody's extreme right, by design she knew, that she should be forced to move, or turn her head to an awkward degree in order to converse with him.

"Have I kept you waiting?" he drawled, knowing full well he had. "My tailor's fault. New fabric samples to choose from, don't you know, and could not make up my mind for the life of me."

"Quite all right," Whitfield said, ever unctuous. "We did not wait so very long."

"He knows exactly how long we have been kicking our heels," Melody informed him. "Exactly as long as intended. Bordering on interminable, but not so long as to drive us to the door."

Burke snorted derisively.

"My dear Lady Bainbridge, I am sure you are mistaken," Whitfield made the mistake of responding.

The sharp-tipped horn of Burke's attention swung in the solicitor's direction. Disdainfully, through his quizzing glass, he eyed the man, as if he insulted his carpet in the same manner the spaniel had the floor. "Who is this?"

"But, sir, you know me. We have spoken. I am Philip Whit—"

"Whoever he is"—Burke waved a dismissive hand—"he is exceedingly rude to address me so freely."

"B-b-but . . ." Whitfield sputtered.

"Have you no memory of my solicitor, Mr. Whitfield?" Melody remained calm. "You have met before, and on more than one occasion."

"Well, I will not have the jackal in my house."

"But, my lord, we did arrange this interview."

"Still he speaks. Out! Out, I say!" Burke pointed toward the door as if Whitfield were but another dog to be ordered from his presence.

Melody rose. "I go if he goes."

Burke shrugged, then settled more comfortably in his chair. "He must leave the room or I refuse to speak to either of you."

"My lady." Tail tucked, on his way toward the door, Whitfield seemed at a loss.

"Not *your* lady at all," Burke contradicted him. "She is, to the contrary, *my* lady."

Melody wanted to follow Mr. Whitfield into the entryway. Indeed, her every instinct urged her to leave the place entire, but she had come to negotiate. Negotiate she would. "You may toss him out if you please," she said with forced nonchalance, "as long as you leave the door open."

"Open?"

"That he might observe our conversation." Her gaze fixed on Whitfield, hoping he understood. "That we might the more easily summon him . . . when an agreement is reached."

"If," Burke corrected her lazily.

She took a deep breath, counted to ten, and let him have the last word, the controlling sentiment.

"*If* we reach an agreement," she amended with a laugh.

Burke's lips thinned on a well-oiled smile. "I am sure we shall manage to come to some sort of understanding. I was ever yours to command." The ingratiating falsehood was intended for the deception of Whitfield rather than out of any goodwill toward her.

She positioned herself in a chair close to the door and stared at the distant prospect of rain-pearled windows and gray velvet clouds, a view far preferable to that of Burke's irksome, fair-weather smile.

Burke rose and circled her chair. Loose-limbed, quiet, and stealthy, he moved to a position behind her, out of her line of sight, worrisome. Like a panther he crept up on her, insinuated his head next to hers, and purred in her ear. "Are you annoyed? You are never in best looks I must warn you, when annoyed, my dear." She flinched away. Too late. His lips he pressed to her cheek. His hands caught her head in too firm a grasp, mashing her face to his mouth. Not a gesture of affection, it was his power over her he displayed. She jerked free, her gaze drawn to the door, where a goggle-eyed Mr. Whitfield watched.

"Regretting now your own insistence that the door should be left open?" Burke's laughter shredded her nerves, the sound not one of amusement. It evidenced contempt. "I shall be on best behavior, my love, otherwise your pet will be in danger of assuming you do not care for me." Languidly, he released his hold on her with trailing hand, the better to negligently disarray her hair.

Mutely, she rose and crossed to the window, tidying strayed strands, her gaze hungry for view of the world outside, a world into which she longed to race. Up to old tricks, he was.

The clink of crystal as a decanter met a glass sent a spasm of fear the length of her spine. Spirits tended to render Burke intractable, to dull the luster of his manners. Liquor roused in him heartless cruelty, a brutish violence.

"What brings you here, my love?" He quaffed a fingerful of brandy in a single swallow, pouring himself another. "I cannot imagine, unless, perhaps, you change your mind?"

She laughed.

"No?" With a trace of irritation he downed half of the second glass. "Nervous that I might win?" He held up his hand, as if to stop her from answering while he took another sip. "No, no. I've got it. You have come to plead leniency for your new love."

Anger smoldered in his tone. She chose her words carefully, no desire to set him aflame. "I came, for no other reason than to rid your life of an annoyance."

"Annoyance?" Restless, he padded about the room,

sipping his drink, pouring another. "But I have so many. Of which would you relieve me?"

"Myself," she said simply. "May we not settle this matter outside of the courts? It would seem a course of action beneficial to both of us."

"How businesslike you sound, my dear. Unwise, really. Business has always been such a bore to me." He yawned broadly. "If this is all the conversation you have to offer, you had best be gone."

"As you wish." She rose and headed for the door.

It was Mr. Whitfield who blurted from the entryway, "Are you not inclined, sir, to have all charges dropped? The matter settled? Outside the courts? Outside of the newspapers?"

"Your jackal yaps, my dear. If he does not desist, I shall be forced to whack him across the snout and shut the door on his howling."

Defeated, she paused a few steps from the threshold. "No need. We will leave you to other amusements."

"So easily you concede." He moved quickly, stepping between her and the door, his back to Whitfield, his arm falling across her shoulder, weighty and oppressive, guiding her back to her chair, a gesture that might appear to be rooted in affection.

Melody allowed him to turn her, to lead her away from the door. "I would not trouble you with anything you have set your mind against."

"You trouble me in leaving too hastily," he announced. "In offering me no more than what I had to begin with."

Melody shrugged. "I offer you relief from a great deal of pointless and unpleasant notoriety."

"Ah, but that is where our opinions differ, my love. There is, to my way of thinking, a wickedly sharp point to this business." His voice sank. Head bent to hers, breath fouled by spirits, the polish of his smile in need of a good waxing, he went on snidely, "As to notoriety, you have far more to lose on that score than I.

Men are so often forgiven their little indiscretions. Women, never."

"The king might not agree with you." She shrugged free from his clutches and sought haven in the nearest chair.

"Ah, the exception to the rule." His voice rose, that Whitfield might bear witness. "You were always fond of contradicting me, but I am surprised you would in any way connect yourself with the queen." His contempt was unmistakable. "Such a tawdry and deplorably public business, conducting a love affair with Bergami, of all people, an Italian without the wherewithal to buy silence. In a tent! On board a ship! Stupid woman."

"This point you spoke of?"

"Point? Ah, yes. The point. Pricked your interest have I? I did used to prick more than that on occasion, Lady Bainbridge, if you will recall."

"I prefer not to." She refused to rise to his baiting.

Displeased, he circled her chair, eyes narrowed, leaning in to whisper heatedly, "I've a great deal to gain from going before the House with my claim, and not all of it the pleasure of vengeance. You must admit I am due some little vengeance . . ." He pushed away from her, and raised his voice, "So uncalled for are your claims against me."

He reached out, so quickly she banged her head against the back of the chair, attempting to avoid him, unsure of his intentions.

He laughed, one finger gently tracing the curve of her cheek, crooking beneath her chin that he might, not so gently, force up her head. "I ask you." His gaze was implacable, unfriendly, chilling in its resolve. He nodded toward the door. "Would a woman who feared brutality pay a social call on the man who beats her?"

She jerked free of him and turned her face from his smile, from the anger his words instilled as he went on relentlessly, "Would she allow him to kiss her, to touch her intimately, in front of a witness, a solicitor no less?"

She closed her eyes, set her chin, and forced her voice to remain unruffled. "This is not a social call."

"What then?"

"It is a business transaction. I bring my man of business with me."

He laughed. "But we conduct no real business, my dear, for neither you nor your jackanapes offer me incentive enough to abandon my current course."

"Yes," she said faintly, rising, red walls closing in. "I am forgetting. You have some point in going before the House."

"Piqued and repiqued your interest, have I? Shall I tell you?"

She advanced on the door, on the wide-eyed interest of Mr. Whitfield. She knew better than to exhibit interest in Burke's motivation. He would never tell her if convinced she cared to know.

"It seems a pointless bother, knowing your reasons, when you have already stated you have no intention of settling this matter in a gentlemanly fashion. No need to show me out. I know the way."

"You've no interest in hearing how all of this applies to the Earl of Erroll?"

That stopped her, as nothing else might, but she refused to turn and face him. "What can you want of him other than a childish, spiteful revenge for sins never committed?" Even as she said it, the simple truth surfaced. "Money!" Her head swiveled that she might judge his reaction. "Is it his money you are after?"

"Have you only just grasped the truth of it?" He laughed heartily. "You *are* a slow top, my dear. Of course money figures into it. It figured prominently in my reasons for asking for your hand, did it not?"

"I was fool enough to believe you loved me."

"Were you? Silly girl. I shall look for a similarly obtuse intellect in my next wife, and a larger dowry."

"You have no other option. An intelligent woman

will not allow you to have her, or her money." She pushed past Whitfield blinded by the darkness of the entryway. "Tibalt," she called. "My cloak and hat, if you please."

Burke lunged, silent, dangerous—Mr. Whitfield tossed aside in the wake of his sudden advance.

"I say!" His objection her only warning, Burke was on her in an instant, her arm caught in an all too familiar grip, his voice low and dangerous. "I am not yet done with you."

Melody allowed no trace of terror to give her words pause, despite the bruising squeeze of Burke's grip. "We are done, Burke—completely done. Surely you see that. I have nothing left. You have taken all there is to be had of me."

Tibalt appeared, his face a studied blankness, hats and cloaks ready for the donning.

Burke's grip tightened. "You are wrong, my precious. There is something more I would have of you, and in return I will give you your every heart's desire, will settle out of court, will leave you to your own devices, will wish you every happiness with this earl of yours."

Vicious, his voice, and yet it captured her attention with such a promise. He knew he had. With a self-satisfied smirk he released her, turned his back on the ruffled Mr. Whitfield, and sauntered into the drawing room—a snake mesmerizing rodents with its sway.

Trapped by her own hope, she trailed after him. "What? What would you have of me?"

"Two things." He rounded on her and bent his head as if to a lover. Smoothly, his arm took possession of her waist. To the window he drew her, well out of the range of Whitfield's hearing. "I would have a lump sum off this earl of yours, a substantial settlement. I am sure his pockets are plump enough. A little wheedling, my dear. I am sure you can coax him to it."

She longed to pull away, but feared doing so would set him against her, reverse his mind on these matters that meant so much, and so she withstood the temptation to fling his arm away, considering the humiliation he requested. Could she go to Dunstan Hay, explain this dreadful request, beg for money in exchange for her freedom? The idea revolted, and yet she could not turn her mind completely against it without hearing the whole.

"Two things," she reminded him. "You said two things you would have of me. What is the second?"

He turned her, his hands too free at her waist and shoulders. He smiled and said nothing. The light in his eyes, the insinuation of his mouth, was familiar. Frighteningly so. "Can you not guess, my dear?"

She stood frozen, inwardly cringing, her hands desperate to be free. Her gaze drifted to the still life of dead game on the bloodred wall. She did not want to guess, did not want to remember how she had first been trapped by his gentle touch, by innuendo, by just such suggestive smiles.

"I've no idea," she said warily, palms gone damp. "You are too clever for me."

He smiled and let the words hang between them, as if he savored them, as if he debated with himself whether or not to tell her. "A little thing, really," he said at last. "You are still my wife. You bear my name. I am sure you will understand I might have some trouble remaining cordial in negotiations with Erroll if I believed he cuckolds me even as he hands over payment for the privilege. I would have you shelter beneath my roof until the money arrangements are made final."

The workings of his mind revolted her. The idea of returning to this house, no matter the reason, made jelly of her knees.

He leaned close, his breath fetid. "It would be no more than a night or two. A final night or two. Our last taste of one another, if you will, before we spit each other out and move on to more appetizing delights."

Her stomach knotted; her back and neck went rigid.

To place herself once again within his grasp contradicted all that she had promised herself. His only purpose in taking her in again was to prove his possession of her to Dunstan Hay.

"Have we an agreement?" he asked. "At such small cost may we both have what we desire."

Small cost. Was it really? Why then could she neither nod, nor spit forth a simple yes?

"Well?" he prodded. "What say you?"

She backed away from the stifling cloud of his cologne, the sweated palm that grasped her waist, the fingers that would touch her hair.

"Would you refuse me?" His voice turned ugly. He grabbed at her shoulder, his grip too hard. More bruises, mild punishment for flouting his will.

"A generous offer, Burke," she choked out. "But I would give it thought before I agree."

"You always were the contrary one, my love." His every endearment was uttered with a biting anger, a latent rage, an additional squeeze, to remind her of past violence. "Always slow to see the sense of things, never any good at driving a bargain. You ought not take too long to respond, sweeting. This offer may not please me tomorrow."

"Perhaps there is summat you would have o' me instead."

She thrilled to hear his voice. Dunstan Hay stood framed in the doorway, unrelieved of hat or overcoat, glistening with rain.

Mr. Whitfield peered past him.

Mr. Tibalt's voice was to be heard, informing him tonelessly, "The master, sir, is not at home to callers."

Dunstan Hay—he had never seemed more welcome, more handsome, more whole and hale and desirable, and yet fear clutched her throat, her heart, her gut. He did not know the lion's den into which he stepped. He did not know the man that Burke was, what he wanted, what he was capable of doing to get it.

She would have stepped toward him, but Burke yet

had bruising hold of her shoulder. She could not lightly shake him loose.

Burke eyed his uninvited guest, a calculating light in his eyes. "You! What do you do here, Scotsman? You are not welcome. You have interfered quite enough with my marriage. Can you not see you interrupt a reconciliation?"

Burke whirled her swiftly into his arms, caught her off guard, and pressed his unwelcome lips to hers.

Revolted, she fought his embrace. Shoving herself free of his kiss, reacting in a blind rage, she struck his cheek a stinging blow—the first time she had ever hit him.

Burke stepped back a pace, laughing. "And I am the one accused of violence." He addressed his audience at the door even as he reached out to grab Melody by the wrist. "Come, sweeting. Kiss and make up. All's forgiven."

"No!" she cried, struggling against his brutal grip. "Let go. You are hurting me."

"Let her go!" Dunstan leapt into motion, his target Burke, who, anticipating his reaction, flung Melody to the floor and raised from his pocket a pistol. He aimed it at Dunstan's heart.

Chapter Nineteen

Dunstan slid to a stop, the barrel of the gun perilously close to his chest. It looked much larger up close.

"Perhaps revenge would suffice," Lord Bainbridge said, his tone, even his manner, oddly polite. "You tempt me sorely, you do, Scotsman." He said it rationally, without heat, as if they discussed the tying of a neckcloth or the snip of fate's scissors on the string of existence.

Dunstan dared not look at Melody. He had the feeling it would be the last thing he saw if he allowed his eyes to stray. One did not, after all, take one's eyes from a snake when it poised to strike.

Burke laughed, enjoying his position of strength. "Play the hero, my lord, and you beg a hero's demise."

"Don't do it, Burke!" Her voice rose from somewhere near their feet. Too desperate she sounded, on the brink of tears.

Bainbridge smiled a dreadful smile. "Do you hear?" he asked with a sneer. "She begs for your life. The hero, who has rushed to save her, finds himself in need of rescuing."

From the door Mr. Tibalt said, "He is unarmed, sir."

Bainbridge shrugged. "Easily remedied. Give him a knife, Tibalt. A butter knife if you please."

Tibalt's voice was even, rational, emotionless, "You will hang for it, sir."

Melody laughed, and with her laughter broke the

awful thread of tension. "I should happily see you hanged, Burke."

Burke ignored her. "The bitch has a sharp tongue," he said conversationally to Dunstan, lowering the gun. "Are you sure you want her? Pretty enough, I'll grant you, but no great prize between the sheets. Perhaps you have already sampled her wares and find them to your liking? There is no accounting for taste."

Dunstan said nothing. Turning his back negligently on Burke and his pistol, he offered Melody a hand, restored her to her feet, and responded in much the same tone. "If she is no longer palatable to you, my lord, perhaps you would consider negotiating to rid yourself of her company?"

He could not look at Melody. His approach was not aimed at pleasing her. He hoped only for resolution with this man and his mercurial temper.

Burke pocketed the pistol, turned to a mirror, a bit of brightness against the scarlet, straightened his neckcloth, and said calmly, "You wish to buy her favors from me, then? You know that is the best you can ever expect to have of her. The law will not allow me to cast her aside entire, and the Church will not allow you to marry her, even should she win her case, which is, I would warn you, based on a packet of the most insidious of lies."

"Lies that work to your advantage if you would cast her aside."

Melody stood very still, her gaze intent upon the two of them. Dunstan could feel the heat of it.

Bainbridge's gaze tripped from the one to the other of them, the curve of his lips one of satisfaction. "To cast her aside like a tuppenny whore little benefits me, sir. Changes next to nothing. We have lived separately for the greater part of two years. I have carried on my life as pleased me, as has she if you are any indication as to her habits."

"What would be of benefit to you, sir?"

"A bribe?" Bainbridge's eyes gleamed, though whether from rage or greed, Dunstan knew not.

He drew from the inner pocket of his coat a red-brown folio of papers tied with black ribbon. "What if I were ready to provide you with some sort of remuneration? If I could, in fact, free you to remarry?"

Bainbridge studied his nails, as if the folio were of no great interest. "Smitten, are you? How much is the minx worth to you? It would depend, to a great degree, on the sums involved. I found her a poor bargain, really. She does not care for wifely duties. Will not spread her legs with anything other than resignation. Buyer beware! I have had far better for free."

Melody would hear them out no more. He could not blame her. Who else would have borne so long such insult? He hated this haggling, and yet there seemed no decent way to deal with a man who had not a single thread of decency.

It tore his heart to hear her quit the room with a despairing sound. He let her go, did not so much as turn his head to observe her exit. It was Mr. Whitfield followed her onto the street, calling out to her that surely she did not wish to walk in the rain.

Grimly, he shut away his concern for her. Time enough later to seek her out, to apologize for this cruelty, to explain the prize he meant to dangle before her husband. The important business of their futures must be concluded here, today, in this very moment, if at all possible.

Sudden movement, a blur of it peripherally. Dunstan dodged Bainbridge's swing.

"Come now, my lord. I've a proposition you would hear," he said as evenly as one could while dancing a hasty retreat.

Bainbridge laughed, and launched another facer. "I've no wish to listen to your proposition and every desire to bloody you."

Dunstan blocked the second swing. "You've more to gain by listening."

"Have I now?" With an aggressive lunge Bainbridge backed Dunstan into a wall. The impact of their bodies sent a painting of dead birds crashing to the floor at their feet. Bainbridge paid it no mind. He had eyes only for Dunstan, whom he pressed to the wall in place of the painting.

"I'm listening," he said, grabbing Dunstan's hair, that he might, with a bit of head banging, pin his guest more completely to the bloodred damask. "Be swift, Scot. I shall be kind enough to listen only as long as you remain standing." With every word, by way of his hair handle, he banged Dunstan's head.

Driving both hands swiftly upward, Dunstan thrust aside Bainbridge's hold, pushing away, dodging the real attack as it came from below the belt rather than above. He took the knee against his thigh rather than his tender organ, and deftly hooked his boot heel behind Burke's only supporting ankle. With a neat punch to the jaw he sent Lord Bainbridge tripping backward, arms pinwheeling.

"Good of you to hear me out," Dunstan said tersely.

Burke glared at him. He was breathing hard as he adjusted the set of his coat, shot his cuffs, and straightened his neckcloth. "I can think of nothing you might say that would interest me, Scot."

"Nay? Can you not? Not even if you would be free to marry again, to start over, to rebuild both family and reputation?"

Stiff-legged, Bainbridge edged to Dunstan's right, his attitude one of assessment. "That is what *you* want. What *she* wants! And I am in no mood to grant either of you favors."

Dunstan turned as he turned, wary of his approach despite the absence of threatening moves.

Burke's expression was completely benign as he closed the gap between them, fingering his tousled hair into place. "I would much rather uncork your claret." With sudden, violent purpose he swung not a fist, but the back of his hand at Dunstan's face.

Startled, Dunstan jerked away—not fast enough. Bainbridge's outstretched fingers glanced jarringly off the end of his nose, I in the explosion of pain, the fluid nonchalance of the movement, there came a blinding moment of clarity. Just such violence had this man perpetrated against Melody. Dunstan was sure of it. He retreated from the unexpected attack, rage rising, an ill-contained rage against this man, who so casually handed out pain.

"Would ya' no' clear your debts, man?" he shouted, ready to promise this man the moon if he might keep Melody safe as a result. His anger added hard edge to the promise. "I can provide you with the means."

His rage threatened to undo him, threatened to interfere with his best intentions. The need to contain that rage took him to the far side of the room, away from the temptation of dimming Bainbridge's daylights. "Can you nae stand to see your obligations paid off, your name cleared, perhaps an annuity set aside for the future?"

"Another man's leavings are worth so much to you?" Bainbridge purred, his manner elegant, playful, dangerous. "Have you Scots no taste for cleaving virgins, that you would take a woman already broken to the saddle, whip, and spur of another rider?"

He stalked about the room, his territory, brushing up against his things, grooming his hair with a rake of his claws. "I had heard rumor you are a warlike race. And yet I get the feeling"—a killed-the-canary smile tugged his lips—"you've so little violence in you it pains you even to the breaking of a hymen."

With a snarl Dunstan launched himself at Bainbridge, fists flailing, a red mist before his eyes. Locked in a violent embrace, the two danced across the room, slamming into a table. It squealed a protest as wooden legs skated across the hardwood floor. Off balance, a candle leapt from the uncertain surface, bleeding wax on table, wall, and floor as it took a header, extinguishing itself in a flurry of sparks. The waxy odor of its death hung about the room.

The rug curled fearfully from the scrabbling of their boots. A chair fell onto its back with a hair-raising screech, lay frozen, legs in the air. Rage whirled around it, tripped over it, kicked at it, shoved it into a corner, scarred and beaten.

From the doorway came feeble attempts to intervene. Mr. Whitfield huffed out, "I say. I say," though what he would say was not immediately self-evident.

"My lord, this accomplishes nothing," Tibalt bleated. The mirror crashed to the floor. "And damages a great deal."

The words fell on deaf ears.

A stool dropped to its knees, furniture in supplication. No mercy. Crushed beneath the building rage, splintered beyond repair, it vomited stuffing onto the floor as rage reached a crescendo, breaking knuckles, bruising mouths.

Daylight waning, the firelight cast in flickering shadows an ungainly waltz upon the wall, the dance of two men locked in a whirl of jabs and blows that wound down at last, the participants too exhausted to continue, two men more beaten than the furniture, bruised, winded, spattered crimson, one on his knees, the other supine.

"I will never give her to you," Burke wheezed. He lay flat on his back, unmindful of torn coat and bloodied shirt front, completely winded. He addressed the ceiling, which would appear to fascinate him. "She is mine! My name marks her. Mine!" The words began and ended on a groan. "Take your money, your annuity"—he spat out a tooth—"and your bleeding Scottish arrogance and get out of my house, adulterer." The words trickled like the blood from his lips.

Clutching the wall, Dunstan rose. His nose ran blood. His left eye was swelling shut. The end of his disarrayed neckcloth served as hankie. He towered over his bruised and bloodied foe, chest heaving. "I . . ." There seemed so little breath within him. " . . . am no . . ." Every word took such effort. " . . . adulterer."

"You lie!" Bainbridge said wearily.

"Nay, now." He exhaled heavily, gathered his every reserve, and swaying, planted his boot in the soft spot beneath Bainbridge's chin. "I'll no' have you call me a liar."

Bainbridge grabbed the boot, heel and toe—but had not the energy to cast him aside.

"Easy it would be, sir." Dunstan concentrated on spitting out the words, on maintaining his balance. "Simple to step on your windpipe as you lie. Cut off your wind and all lies are ended. Here. Now."

From the doorway Whitfield warned, "An actionable offense, my lord! I do advise against it."

Tibalt cleared his throat. " 'Deed, sir. Not the wisest course."

Dunstan paid them no mind.

Bainbridge spoke thickly through bloodied lips, no trace of fear in his eyes. "My wife," he wheezed, every word deliberate, labored, "will watch you hang if you do!"

The words vibrated through the sole of Dunstan's boot.

Melody. Mention of her gave him pause.

"Would that she were widow rather than wife," he said gruffly, removing his boot, grown heavy, from its cradle. "As much as you do tempt me, sir, I canna' steal the breath from you, no matter how foul it may be."

"Excellent decision, sir," Tibalt said.

"Weakling!" Burke taunted. "Were the roles reversed, you would be drawing breath no more."

"Aye. You're a selfish bastard, Bainbridge," Dunstan said sadly. "A bloody selfish fool with little idea of how precious life can be."

"You shall not have her!" Bainbridge growled.

"Nor shall you." Dunstan laughed, his wind returning, the ringing in his ears receding. "Do you nae ken? You canna' give her to me. Only she can give herself away, man. If your wife chooses to gi' herself to me, as she chose once to gi' herself to you, I am fortunate, indeed, and possessed of enough wisdom and self-control not to abuse the offering." He held out his hand. "Will you get up now, man? Can we no' reach an agreement? Or do you prefer to lie aboot all day?"

Burke Bainbridge rolled away from the outstretched hand. "Be gone!" he snarled. "You were never welcome here."

Chapter Twenty

Disheartened, hat dripping, shoes soaked, Melody wandered the streets, in no hurry to return to the rooms she and Blanche shared. She felt like damaged goods, like chattel, an item of barter, no better than a man's horse, or dog, or mistress. Nothing she did or said could change her circumstances, nothing could wash away the stain of her own stupidity in having wed Burke Bainbridge.

Damn the man! Damn all men. How could Dunstan Hay have said the things he had?

Drenched and yet warmed by anger and shame, she turned into South Audley Street to the tune of a man's uncultured voice raised to shout at one of the gates guarding a large house, his tone derisive. "How does Mrs. Innocence get on?"

He was one of two wet fellows, an empty barrow between them, farmers, perhaps. They had the look of the country in the cut and color of their mud-splattered clothes, in the length of their stride and the set of their wide-brimmed hats.

The second fellow doffed his hat and held it level with his mouth, pinkie extended, as if it were a tea cup. "I would suppose she is at this time of day tippling with some of the humbug Italians." He poured rain from his imaginary teacup and planted it once again upon his balding pate. "Not out in the rain, as we are, making a living by the sweat of our brows."

"No," his companion agreed, "but she does know how to hold up her skirts, our Caroline." Raising the tail of his coat about his waist, he thrust forward his hips with rude suggestion.

"For shame!" Melody shouted, and louder, her ire rising hotly with the words, "shame on the two of you!"

They turned and caught sight of her. The one with his coat hiked stifled a guffaw, letting go his tails, the pantomime ended. The other punched his sashaying companion on the shoulder and shrugged down into his collar, as if ashamed to show face.

The barrow was set in motion. The two followed it down the street, their laughter muffled, but not extinguished.

Slowing her steps, Melody advanced to the spot where they had made such brazen spectacle of themselves. The house looked much like any other. And yet it was not just any who suffered such public abuse.

The damp suddenly uncomfortable, too cold, Melody passed the windows that looked out onto the street, her eyes drawn to a flutter of curtain. There, on the first floor, a woman stared at her. Dark hair framed her face. Could it be the queen peering out through rain-spotted pane?

This was Cambridge House, the queen's new residence. She had been asked to remove herself from Bradenburg House in St. James's Square, loaned to her during the course of the divorce proceedings. It was said she and her incompetent staff left uninhabitable chaos in their wake. They had ruined carpets, curtains, bed linens, and most of the silver.

A queen without a palace, and her husband ill-disposed to provide her with enough means to live in the state befitting her rank.

Inspired by a memory, the touching memory of Dunstan Hay doffing his hat at the Wells, Melody stopped to cut a dripping curtsey. She looked up to see a pale, plump hand raised to touch the glass, the dark head bowed as if with grief. The hand fell away, the woman withdrew from the window. The curtain fell still.

Chilled, lonely, more disheartened than ever, Melody headed home, at least to the place that passed for home here in London, the apartments she shared with Blanche.

Blanche turned from packing a trunk as Melody entered—turned as a startled mouse will turn, eyes wide and dark with fear. "Melody!" she cried, handkerchief flying to her mouth. "Dear God, my dear. Where have you been? Worried sick, I was." She stuffed the handkerchief between her lips and wrenched it out again, blinking with puffy-eyed surprise. She had been crying.

"So sorry, Blanche. Did not mean to worry you."

"Come in. Come in. You are drenched to the skin!"

Stripping herself of dripping attire, dropping it in sodden piles as she went, Melody searched in growing dismay the mountains of clothes that had been emptied onto the bed from wardrobe, cupboard, and shelf.

"Do you mean to leave?" she asked, dismayed.

"I do," Blanche asserted, tearing up again. "I will not stay in this dreadful city another day. My cottage stands empty too long. My kitty . . ." Tears swamped her voice. She daubed desperately with her hankie, turned to the case, jabbed a pair of stockings into the corner, blew her nose, and turned back. "Mrs. Weller is perfectly capable, of course. But, I do miss Puss. I do not know what I would do if she ran away."

Melody unearthed a pile of linen, toweled herself dry, and slipped into the first dress she laid hands on. "Comb?" she said, planting herself in front of the fireplace, throwing her hair over her head, that it might drip onto the carpet, instead of her back.

"A comb. Of course. A comb," Blanche muttered, gathering herself together in the search for something so ordinary, so necessary. Thrusting it into Melody's hand, she bent to the fire, turning the rod that held the kettle into the flames, that the water might boil, and bustled about again among her cases and trunks, muttering. "Tea. You will need to down something hot at once, else you will surely take chill."

Melody watched her nervous flutter as she combed wet tangles from her hair. "What has put you in such a pet?" she asked when Blanche, tea caddy and cups located, returned to tend the kettle.

Blanche sniffed, her arms crossing over, wrapping round her chest. Not from cold, her cheeks had gone pink with the fire's heat. "I am going, Melody, my dear. Nothing you can say will convince me to stay."

"You are serious," Melody said calmly. "I can see you are. But, dearest Blanche, I am completely at sea as to why you should decide this so suddenly. Have you received disturbing news from home? Have I said or done something to upset you?"

"Not you!" Blanche's voice rose in her distress.

Melody abandoned her hair and clasped her cousin's shoulders, recognizing the flinch as she did so—the averted eyes.

"Has *he* been here? Was it Burke convinced you to go?"

Blanche collapsed in her arms like a parasol, tears raining. "Oh, Melody, my love. He came! Came here!"

"Burke did?"

A sodden nod.

"When? I have just come from him."

"It was this morning." Blanche gratefully accepted a fresh handkerchief snatched from one of the cases at Melody's feet. "Just after you left for Mr. Whitfield's office."

"That snake. What did he do here? What said he to put you in such a state?"

"Made himself very much at home, he did. Seemed as urbane and polite as always when he first arrived. But there was a rage in him, Mellie, a meanness I have never been privy to before. I know you warned me as to his character, but I never knew . . . I am sorry . . . I never really knew . . ." Her face was awash with tears now. Her voice tripped and stumbled over words made clumsy by emotion.

"Did he dare to hurt you?"

The question sent Blanche into a fresh fauceting. As she sobbed, she nodded, and then, as if confused, shook her head. "Not really. Did not even raise his voice. Just went about the place emptying wardrobes, suggesting it would be best for all concerned if I were to go. You know how he is."

"Yes. All too well."

"He said I was a troublemaker, a busybody meddler with my nose poked in places it did not belong. He said I must be careful it was not . . ." She tried to snap her finger, but failed, and in the failure fell once more to wetting her collar.

Melody comforted her with a cooing sound and a fresh handkerchief. "Made you think he would do the snapping, did he?"

"Oh God bless, Melody. He took me by the shoulders. Shook me, he did. Said that your marriage might have been saved but for me. A home wrecker, he said." Tears again, both handkerchiefs sodden with them. "His eyes." She dabbed at her own, blew her nose, and cast about her gaze, as if his eyes were on her yet. "There came a madness in them."

"I know."

"Left me weak-kneed."

"I know, I know."

"Ready to agree to anything he asked of me."

"And he asked you to leave."

"Threatened me that I should regret it mightily if I did not. Said the two of you must settle your differences without my butting in."

"He was right."

"No!"

"Yes." Melody would brook no argument. "You must go and feed your cat, and see that the cottage is ready to receive me. I shall stay only as long as it takes to finish this nasty business, and with an easier heart if I know you are safely tucked away in the country."

"But, my dear. I would have you come with me."

"Burke would only follow if I did."

Chapter Twenty-one

He waited for her on the steps of the house where she and Blanche lodged, beaten, bloody, one eye swelling shut, countless muscles aching, lips and knuckles torn. His head throbbed, his nose, his jaw, his very teeth ached. He left red splats on the steps. Old blood, dried blood, rewetted, it washed away in the misting rain. Chilled, bruised, and weary, he would wait for her, would share with her the contents of the folio.

"Dunstan?" she exclaimed at first sight of him. "Dear Lord! Are you all right?"

"Right as rain," he muttered, wincing as his split lip tore anew. His heart lifted at the sight of her.

She paused on the step beneath his, her expression one of deepest concern. Slipping off one glove, she tentatively caressed the puffed-up flesh about the eye that saw the least of her.

He flinched and pulled back.

"My husband did this to you?"

He frowned, sniffed, tongued the tear in his lip, and said with undeniable satisfaction, "He is hurting as much, if not more."

"Is that supposed to make it all right? Surely you must realize I detest violence. An intelligent man does not try to best a brutal man at his own game. You will not beat a violent man with violence. There are other ways, better ways, surely."

The disappointment in her expression, her voice, the withdrawal of her hand as she stepped past on her way to the door was almost too much for him.

With great effort, and more than a little pain, he rose, prepared to leave.

"You will come up," she said without turning. No question of his refusing.

He followed her in and up the stairs, head down, one step after the other, every inch of him protesting movement.

She fumbled with the second key, the one that opened her door. She seemed a trifle brisk as she swept in, pulling her hat from her head, shrugging her cloak from her shoulders.

"I shall just put on the kettle for some hot water. Sit down. It may take me a moment to find some gauze and sticking plaster."

He sat by the fire, thought better of it. Heat would only heighten his pain. Rising, he moved to a more distant chair. It was piled high with hats.

The room was a mess, clothes thrown about as if a great wind had blown through the place. A trunk sat open upon the floor, half packed.

She was leaving! He blinked his good eye, gaze roving, seeking some evidence his deduction was incorrect. How could she simply pack up and leave?

"Where is Blanche?" he asked. The rooms were too still. He knew she was not there, and yet she must be. Melody would never have asked him in if she were not.

"Gone," she said simply, breezing through the room, gauze in one hand, scissors in the other, dumping the contents of one of the chairs onto the floor, directing him to sit.

"Gone? Where?"

"Home. It was to the posting house I went. To see her safely off." She brought clean linen next, and a basin for the water, which she poured steaming from the kettle, testing it with the tip of a finger, adding cold from a pitcher until she was satisfied.

"Without you?"

"Evidently." She chuckled.

How he loved the sound, and yet it made no sense.
"You asked me in."

"Again you state the obvious. I could not leave you
to bleed on the doorstep in the rain, now could I?"

She plunged linen into the water and stood before
him to wash the blood from his nose and eye. Silent
and efficient, she moved about him, her hands cool
and soothing, her skirt brushing his knees, his thighs,
as she daubed at cuts and bruises, as she checked his
scalp and applied a plaster to his ear.

Her breasts, lush temptation, hung before him at
eye level, though only his good eye could do justice to
the spectacle. Her neckline proved a distraction, the V
between her breasts heady with the scent of a heathery perfume. He longed to rest his forehead against
her ripe softness, longed to nuzzle nippled curves. Instead he sat silent and submissive, his gaze following
her every movement, his bruised flesh receptive to
her every soothing touch.

That touch, so sweet, so longed for, closed both of
his eyes on occasion, tears welling, stopped his
breathing, slowed the very beat of his heart. His entire
concentration centered on the play of her fingertips.

She seemed completely comfortable, relaxed in
tending to him, but her calm was no more than a facade. She jumped at one point when his leg came into
contact with hers. She laughed nervously at her own
skittishness, laughed, too, when she asked him to remove his blood-spattered coat, to strip off his shirt,
that she might salve his bruises and check for cracked
ribs.

He stood—made the attempt. His knuckles were
too swollen, several flayed raw. It was up to her to
finish the unbuttoning, she who pulled from his
shoulders the coat, his waistcoat. With shaking hands
she unwound his neckcloth, unfastened more buttons,
and lifted his shirttail from his breeches. Pushing the
fabric away from his torso and shoulders, lifting it
over his head, she pulled the sleeves free. He did not
help too much in the removal. All of his clothes and

most of hers would have followed in a rush had he moved a muscle.

The purpose of her hands, the uneasy hitch that interrupted her breathing now and then as she bared him, led him to the brink of lost control. With an unsteady inhalation, with a stiffness not confined to abused joints and bruised muscles, he allowed her to do with him as she would. She offered him tincture of laudanum to dull the pain. He drank it down for her. She raised the basin of warm water from the floor and instructed him to plunge both battered hands into it. He did as she asked, bore the pain without murmur. Not a word slipped from his lips. He would have cried out his love for her had he uttered a single syllable.

It was she who broke his resolve, his self-control and better intentions—she who took away the water, ran searching hands over every rib before declaring them sound. It was she who applied salve to his back, shoulders, and stomach, her fingers fleet, gentle, and all too provocative. She it was who kissed first his bruised brow and then, ever so gently, his swollen eye, and finally with feather softness, the side of his lip that was not split.

He sat mute beneath her ministrations, motionless and unresponsive, until her lips brushed his. With the moan of a man overcome, he slid hands about her waist and pulled her to him. She came without protest. The plush softness of her muslin-covered breasts met briefly his bare chest, skimming lightly the length of his torso, as she slid to a kneeling position between his thighs.

He bent to return her kisses, feather-soft his mouth on hers, but hungry, his appetite mounting, dulling pain. His lip split, hers uncertain, like the wings of moths drawn to the light of their feelings, the heat of their breath, the glow of long-suppressed desire, they danced together, apart, together again.

His mouth on hers grew more persistent, despite its recent abuse. The sweetness of conquest, of surrender, overrode his aches and pains. He was stiff and achy, his provocation temptation, desire, the proposed fulfillment of both. His hands sought out the hills of buttocks and thigh, the sweet valley of her waist, rising to rib ridges, higher, her breath coming faster, to scale the peaks and mountains in turmoil, rising, falling, the rhythm tumultuous, the satin promise of her hillsides provoking volcanic heat within him.

His hands pleased her. He could hear pleasure in her sudden gasps, in the dreamy carol of her sigh, in the liquid ripple of soft laughter. He read approval in the glowing depths of her eyes, in the reciprocal pressure of her hands, beckoning—seeking—in the provocative, heathery smell of desire rising warm and sweetly musky between them.

It seemed only natural that she should rise, removing pins from her hair, shaking it out like cloth of gold to cover them as his hands rose, slid her shoulders bare of fabric, her nipples echoing the hard rise of his organ as he closed his mouth hotly over the fabric covering one tumescent hillock. Back arching, she shuddered, breast thrusting into the heated wetness, not away.

Without words—no words were needed—they moved together in perfect concert. She straddled his knees when he lifted her skirts, her hands moving without hesitation, gracefully unfastening the buttons that held fast his breeches. She sought and freed the throbbing heart of him, stroked the rigid length once, and rocking forward in his lap, her hand to guide him, with a moan of profound contentment, sank home.

She found, in the bliss of their lovemaking, a contentment of place, time, and company that banished loneliness, fear, and all sense of tomorrows. There was only the moment, the sheer contentment of it. The fullness of her heart left room for nothing else.

She nested in his arms and burrowed against his chest. He nested between her thighs, burrowing deeper. The chair was home to them, the floor a haven.

With the sparest vocabulary they crooned their mutual need, desire and satisfaction in a sotto voce chorus of yeses and an occasional heartfelt acknowledgment to the deities who might be responsible for the heaven into which they ascended.

She swam in the ethereal, swam the musky Milky Way of their lovemaking, entirely comfortable in their mutual nakedness, in the disposition of legs twined, in the splay of her hair across his chest, in the swollen, throbbing contentment of her lips, upper and nether. Insatiable, his tongue prodded her for more, always more, a heated, probing insistence. She opened herself up to him, sliding from the peak of arousal to the warm depths of sleep's oblivion.

"I never knew it could be like this." Her muffled words, joy sighed into the feather mattress, evoked laughter, and then a groan as his amusement tested recently abused muscles.

"Come to me, my lady Melody." Her name from his lips was such sweetness she must kiss them. He drew her close, his mouth as honeyed as the damp between her thighs, where slowly, sticky sweet, he rocked her, his voice gentle, reverent, his hands tracing pathways from shoulder to thigh.

"It has never," he whispered, his voice as gentle as the rocking, "since the dawn o' time, been like this before."

Her back arched. Her hips rose to meet his.

But for one moment, one black moment in the darkness, when she allowed her doubts, her fears, to surface, they wrapped themselves in a cocoon of safety, of completion, of perfection. But for that single exception, there was for the length of a night, no past, no troubled tomorrows, only the white-hot blur of the moment, the velvet warmth of flesh against flesh, the honeyed heat of breath into breath.

Doubt surfaced at four in the morning, the darkest

hour before dawn. He stirred beside her as she turned with a sigh to stare bleakly at the blackness above them.

"What troubles you, my love?" he asked when she did not immediately curl into the shelter of his arms.

"The future," she said, her voice small, uncertain.

"What of it? We shall hie away to Scotland." His accent was thicker than usual, evidence, perhaps, of agitation. "There to live happily ever after."

"As what?"

"As husband and wife, o'course."

"But we cannot be married."

"Mayhap not, in the eyes of the law. In my heart we shall be forever joined."

She turned to him and touched the softly curling mat of hair on his chest. "It will matter to our children, should we be so blessed."

"It need no'. I've money enough to see they never want for anything."

"Can you buy them respect? Can you buy them your good name?"

"They will carry my name. Shall be well provided for in the event of my death, but do we not race ahead of ourselves? You have yet to say you wish to go away wi' me."

"Every wish." She closed her eyes, shutting out the darkness for more darkness. She could not shut out her fear so easily.

"Follow that wish," he whispered. "We shall be the happiest couple in Scotland."

"For how long? Can you state unequivocally that you will never regret having cast aside your inheritance, your family's unsullied name, the future of your offspring, all for the love of one woman?"

"You are far too serious for the middle o' the night, love. Can you find nothing to laugh at in the irony of our situation?"

"Laugh?"

"Aye. There is something vastly amusing in the way the laws of God and country do work to keep you bound to a man who would beat you and apart from another who loves you, who will cherish you with his dying breath. Come. Give me a laugh. You are always one for recognizing the humor in man's folly."

She could not laugh, but she did worm closer to him in the bed, fitting her body to his. She did not plague him with further questions, merely clung to the warmth of him and allowed sleep to carry her away from her worries.

She woke to a weak slice of morning light filtering through the curtains, tomorrow caught up to her, time and its troubles manifesting themselves in the mound of man who shared her sheets, a man unbound to her in any way but the fragile ties of their mutual feeling. She had entrusted herself and her future to him completely—too completely.

The union they had shared—incredible, indescribable, perfect—their implicit trust, their bond was to the law, the Church, and the society of their peers criminal congress, an unspeakable sin—a matter guaranteed to evoke intrigued whispers, sly looks, witty innuendo. In the light of day her love became a tawdry thing—tumbled sheets, a throbbing rawness in the most sensitive areas of her body, and a man asleep in her bed. A longing beset her to reach out, to run fingers along the intimately familiar curves and planes of the body next to hers. Hard to recapture the feeling of safety, of security, of coming home. It seemed an elusive dream with his eyes shut to her, his bruised arms leaden and unfriendly with sleep, his desire shrunken and limp between his legs.

She slid from the bed, heavyhearted, alone, afraid, uncertain of the future, the questions from the dead of night still plaguing her.

She could not give herself up to bliss only to wake to the harsh light of reality every morning for the rest of her days. She could not go to Scotland as Dunstan wished her to, not as his mistress, a fallen woman, a disgrace to family, an unwelcome pariah to neighbors and friends. She could not be happy bringing children into such a world, no matter how incredible the moments of their conception.

She could not, would not submit to Burke.

And yet, where to go? What to do? She turned her back on the lure of Dunstan Hay and gazed at her reflection and beyond it the reflection of Dunstan as he groaned and rolled over. Stealthily, unwilling to wake him, she washed away the scent of their passion, clothed the body he had touched so intimately, and fingered the bruise high on her cheekbone—she had almost forgotten Burke's backhanded reproof.

Yesterday. An eternity had passed since then. She tidied the hair in which her love had buried his nose, praising its texture, its fresh smell. She drew on her hat and her cloak, then hovered briefly bedside, staring down at the fall of his lashes, the boyish cast of his battered countenance, at the purpling skin, once so fair, along his ribs. Had she the strength to survive a life bereft of him, bereft of their passion?

Quietly, regret slowing her steps, she left him— stepping into the misted avenue.

There was only one clear direction left open to her.

Chapter Twenty-two

London, November 21, 1820

She went to Lady Hay—knew not where else to turn. Veiled, to hide her fresh bruise, Melody knocked at her door, pushed past the servant who answered, and barged in on the woman as she broke fast in the company of several guests: a man, a woman, three wide-eyed boys.

"Lady Hay." She announced her own presence before a cadre of speechless servants, their feet skidding on polished floors in their haste, hard on her heels. "A moment alone, if you please. I would speak to you."

Lady Hay, fork in one hand, lorgnette in the other, eyed her interruption with distaste. "Who dares to barge in on me, uninvited?" With unguarded regret, she rose, relinquished her fork, and, leaning upon her walking stick, addressed her guests. "Pray, do excuse me, Barnard, Gillian. I shall only be a moment."

Joining Melody, she said curtly, her voice hushed, "This way, Lady Bainbridge. It is you beneath that veil, is it not? No one else of my acquaintance goes about with face hidden."

Into a drawing room she led her, a room predominantly blue, remarkable at first glance for its orderliness, and for the portraits gracing the walls—one of Lady Hay, the other of her son. The former Lord Hay was notable only by his absence. Lady Hay closed the door before she said derisively, as if there could be no other explanation, "Come for the money, have you?"

Melody bit back an angry retort. "Not money, my lady. Sanctuary. Assistance."

"Sanctuary? In this house? You are confused, my dear. It is my son offers you sanctuary, not I."

"I am not entirely free to accept your son's generosity. Nor would I care to endanger him."

"Endanger him? Whatever do you mean? Have you no shame, girl? Return to your husband."

"I will not do that." Melody stood uneasily, hands clasped, examining in turn the painting of a younger Dunstan and the inhospitable scowl of the woman whose house she had invaded. She tried to see some commonality between the two.

"Your cousin then. Or has she turned you out?"

Melody sighed. The nose was the same—strong, beakish—the forehead, too, and something about the chin. Nothing else. "Blanche is endangered by my presence," she said. "I would free her of the risks my company engenders."

"Risks? Would you put me in her place then?"

"I would put no one in such a position."

"To what risks do you refer?"

Melody removed her veil and stood motionless while Lady Hay peered at the fresh bruise on her cheek by way of her glass. When it was lowered, Melody bowed her head, drained by the complete absence of empathy with which she had been examined. "My husband dealt me but the one blow this time. My cousin has been threatened with the same. Your son—"

That got her attention. "My son? What about my son? I should have known his absence had something to do with you."

"He has been injured. He fought my husband."

"Where is he? I would go to him," she demanded, the volume of her voice increasing in equal proportion to the disdain of her regard.

"He is fine. Nothing that will not heal. He was sleeping when I left him."

Lady Hay's scorn grew more pronounced. Her lorgnette took a beating against the palm of her hand.

"Sleeping?" Her voice registered nothing but contempt. "He rests even now in your rooms, perhaps? Shameless girl. Why do you come here? To torment me?"

"I come because I am not shameless." Melody enunciated the words carefully, her eyes burning with unshed tears. "I come to beg your assistance."

The door to the drawing room opened, startling them. The gentleman from the breakfast table poked in his head. "Aunt Georgianna. Is aught amiss?"

He spoke with an accent very much like Dunstan's. His features, too, bore resemblance.

Lady Hay waved a peremptory hand. "Go away, Barnard. I've business to attend to."

Barnard eyed Melody with interest. "I didna' mean to be a bother, Auntie, but Jill and I mean to take the lads out for a stroll, perhaps to see the optical illusion of the king and queen we have heard so much about, The Likeness of Eminent Characters."

"Yes, yes, please do. There are any number of sights to keep them entertained."

With a final keen look directed at Melody, Barnard went away.

"My nephew," Lady Hay said. "You will forgive me for failing to introduce you?"

"Of course," Melody snapped, her patience at an end. "You will forgive me for pressing the point. Do you mean to help me, or shall I go away as well?"

Lady Hay seemed for a moment at a loss, but when Melody made a move to leave, her hand flew out. "Do you care for refreshment, Lady Bainbridge? Tea, perhaps?"

He woke to find her gone, the bed empty, the room too still, his body rigid with locked muscles. Every inch of him complained in rising. The night's exertions had numbed all pain at the time, but increased his aches immeasurably now. Cold and naked, he trailed through the puzzling silence. His clothes he found spread out to toast before the fire, the only neatness in a room of chaos. He dressed slowly, with swollen fingers, every minute expecting her arrival. He went to the window to retie his crushed neckcloth, convinced she had stepped out for no more than a moment, a conviction that faded with the morning mist. Minutes and then hours ticked away. He paced the room, stopped pacing to fold her clothing, to hang away dresses. That done he fell to pacing again. His stomach troubled him with its emptiness.

He left as the clock chimed twelve, worried, confused, determined to find her.

She watched and waited until he had gone. Then up the stairs she raced and about the rooms with the energy of one possessed of profound conviction—a conviction she dared not question. Nor did she consider abandoning it, even for a moment. All was packed and ready in less than an hour's time, a hack called for. Without opportunity to draw breath, without a lull in which to think or change her mind, certainly without opening the red-brown folio tied with black string that Dunstan had left propped on the mantel, the words "Gone to look for you" scrawled on the outer flap—she was boarding a post coach bound for Buckinghamshire. It was there Barnard had a bit of land, and on it a property he did not know whether to rebuild or raze.

Melody had been given the task of determining what was best.

It was the housekeeping and management of a country house she had suggested to Lady Hay as a living she would be well suited to. It was recommendation to a living she required, not money. She meant to earn her own. Byngate Manor was the closest thing Lady Hay could come up with on short notice. So it was, in the end, Barnard Hay who provided Melody a destination.

"Ne'er been there," he said when the idea was suggested. "Canna' think why Father invested in a bit o' property so far from Scotland."

"Can you not, Barnard?" Lady Hay had stopped him. "The place is far from Scotland, but convenient to London. Come, come! He and my husband were much the same in their habits."

Barnard looked at her blankly. "He liked to fish. Called the place his angler's nook."

"Ha! Of course he told your mother he was off fishing. But, my dear boy, it was not salmon or pike he was angling after. He lured women to the place—very much in the manner my husband kept a hunting box in Sussex."

Barnard nodded. "I knew about the hunting box. Mother mentioned my uncle's attachment to a woman most unsuitable, but I do not think she knew, at least she could no' allow herself to admit, Father was no better." He was frowning, his thoughts distant when he looked up and realized Melody had heard the whole of a story not meant for a stranger's ears. "I do beg your pardon," he said. "This is beside the point we were after."

"Not so very far from the point at all," Lady Hay said, directing a speaking look at Melody.

She was right. It was not so far from the point.

Melody fixed her eyes on the horizon as the coach rocked its way out of London. She must not think of Dunstan in connection with the bump and sway, concentrated instead on recalling her private conversation with Lady Hay.

"I could not find it within me to leave my husband," Lady Hay had said coolly as she poured their tea. "I think it took great courage for you to do so."

Melody almost scalded her tongue, so amazed was she. She stared at her hostess a moment, confounded, speechless. With those few words the woman before her seemed completely changed.

Lady Hay calmly filled a second cup.

"You did once consider such a course?" Melody had to ask.

"Oh, yes." Lady Hay passed the sugar bowl. "More

than once, and yet, never did I go beyond the contemplation of it."

"Was he cruel to you?"

"Not physically, as your husband appears to have been. Lord Hay was far subtler than that. He never lifted a finger to hurt me, but his tongue, his manner, his attitude were not at all kind. He believed me his inferior in every way. I had no noble blood to boast, no connections within the society he so highly valued. My money was attractive, but I was an embarrassment to him, and he let everyone know it."

"That must have been very trying."

"Yes. On more than one occasion I considered taking the route you have chosen. It would have been simple enough to prove my husband's infidelities."

"What stopped you?"

She laughed and in her amusement, for a moment, looked as young as the portrait behind her. Her gaze fixed on the painting behind Melody. "Why, Dunstan, of course. What would the father do with the son of a mother who had disgraced him with a separation? He would surely have kept him from me. I could not bear that. Too dearly did I love him, you see." Her features seemed to age in an instant.

"Yes, I do see." Melody's heart ached for the young woman in the portrait.

Lady Hay agreed with a nod. "Perhaps better than anyone."

Chapter Twenty-three

London, November 24, 1820

It was in Mr. Mason, Dunstan placed his trust. An ordinary-looking fellow, potbellied and brown—brown hair, brown eyes, unremarkable features. He came highly recommended.

"Wallpaper," he called himself. "I blend in. A man who blends can easily find a body."

"She is alive," Dunstan informed him coolly. "I've no reason to believe otherwise."

"A body live or dead. I did mean no disrespect. I can find her well enough if she remains in London, my lord. You need only give me a list of Lady Bainbridge's known associates."

"Aye." Dunstan began to scribble them down even as the two conversed. "Her husband, o' course."

"Not a widow, then?" Mason did not frown, his features of the immobile, expressionless variety, but a line appeared between his brows, as if he had been offered a puzzle. "And what did you say your relationship is to the woman?"

"I did no' say," Dunstan replied, colder still. With growing irritation he submitted himself to the man's assessment. He had these past few days received undue attention for no more reason than the plum-and-saffron bruises that marked his face. It ought not bother him that this man pried. It was for his prowess in prying he had been hired. "You need to know." He leaned forward, pointing at his face, his words heavy with significance. "Her husband is a volatile man. It was he gave me these."

Mason nodded. "And is he bruised as well, sir?"

"He is."

"I see."

"Do you?" Dunstan could not keep his voice completely level. "She must not return to him, man. Do ye ken? He has given her bruises in the past, just as vile."

"I shall not be getting in the way of his fists, sir," Mason said without emotion, without humor. "Anyone else she might turn to?"

"Her cousin, Blanche. She lives in a cottage in Hertfordshire."

Mason nodded. "Friends? Business associates? Someone within the Church, perhaps? Has she the means to go far?"

Dunstan rubbed his forehead, shook his head, and realized how little he really knew of Melody Bainbridge. "Her lawyer is a Mr. Whitfield. Other than that, I do not know." His voice thinned. "I do not know."

"Do not fret, my lord," Mason said, very businesslike, completely confident. "I shall find her for you, if she is to be found."

Damp and cold, December drizzled slowly away from Melody, who took up residence in the echoing and uncomfortably drafty hulk of a gatehouse in Buckinghamshire—all that remained of the medieval mansion that had once been known as Byngate Manor. Like a mastiff standing guard over a pile of useless bones, the gatehouse sat on squat haunches, a gaping hole between its legs, through which coaches had once been driven. Three stories tall, turreted on every corner, the crenelated towers stuck up like bitten ears. By way of five windows over the riblike remains of the manor, the gatehouse looked out over stockade and stables, their roofs robbed of lead and slate, decades past, for the construction of a local country seat.

This gatehouse led nowhere, guarded nothing. Pale blue, the sightless sockets of the manor house framed the sky. A carpet of grass grew within crumbling walls painted by lichens, mosses, and trailing vines.

It was in this doglike guardian of shattered splendor Melody made herself useful, with the assistance of a single maid, Maddie, a quiet slip of a local girl who spoke but rarely, and who quailed and squeaked at every odd sound to be heard within the creaking walls they thought to save. She was, she said, convinced ghosts walked the grounds.

Ghosts or not, they set to work at once, airing, dusting, and sweeping clean the rooms in which they took up residence. Fires had to be lit, new linens procured, provisions stocked in the bare larder.

Cheerful and biddable, Dan Smith drove a ponycart in from the local village whenever the weather allowed. He brought them provisions, saw to the heavy lifting, and provided fresh wood for the fireplaces. "Ought to pull the place down," he told Melody the first time they met, after she explained her purpose.

"Quite likely you are right," she said. "It is to see if there is any chance of salvaging the gatehouse that I have come."

He shook his graying head and tapped a used plug of tobacco from his clay pipe. "Place is haunted, you know."

"Is it? Maddie mentioned ghosts. I did not take her seriously."

He dug about for a pouch of tobacco and refilled the pipe. "A soldier is said to walk the grounds." The pipe stem waved in the general direction of the stockade. "And a woman in white passes through the rooms above." The pipe stem jabbed in the direction of the gatehouse.

"A woman? Who?"

He jabbed the pipe in the corner of his mouth and spoke through clenched teeth. "Her as jumped from the window." His nod indicated the uppermost floor.

"A singer she was, from London. One of a parade of London women."

"This happened recently?"

Busy with a match, he sucked the fresh tobacco to a glow. "Twenty years gone. It was 'er death stopped the gent from visitin' the place."

"Why did she jump?"

He puffed contentedly, smoke trailing from his lips and nostrils, smoke gathering in an aromatic cloud about his head.

"Got 'er with child is the rumor. But, of course, 'e 'ad a wife and children to go 'ome to. She ought not to have got 'erself in such a position."

"No. I'm sure you are right." Melody studied the window above them, pipe smoke stinging her eyes, blurring her line of vision. His words struck uncomfortably close to home. "Do you think she loved him?" She could not refrain from asking.

He seemed surprised she should wonder. "Dunno. Some sort of passion involved to drive 'er out a window now, wasn't there?"

"I suppose so." A wisp of white passed between her and the window—pipe smoke—and yet it gave her a start. "What a dreadful end. I hope she rests in peace, poor woman."

"Indeed." He chuckled. "We must hope so. Else you shall not find rest yourself while you are here."

Sleepless, uneasy, Dunstan walked the city by night, haunted by memory of her skin, her scent, her heat—the memories a torment. Day after day passed and still no news of her. The weather matched his mood—sullen, clouded, too melancholy to be borne. Leather slapping stone, his hat tugged down against the wet, he plumbed streets and alleyways, riverside and parks, markets and posting houses.

Through throngs he passed, into smoke-filled inns and dance houses he stepped, by way of every riverboat he took passage. He questioned a multitude of strangers: coachmen, bargemen, chairmen, carriers, anyone connected with a conveyance. His palm was ever ready with coin to loosen tongues—tongues that told him nothing. Dark, seamy, and desperate the face of London he uncovered. But no Melody Bainbridge. She was not to be found. Not a trace of her.

His mother's house, by contrast, seemed too full, too warm, too brightly lit. Gillian was there, and Barnard and three of Barnard's boys, rambunctious and contrary. And with them hung laughter and movement and noise. He could not think for the painfully intrusive stab of their happiness. An outsider looking in on their togetherness, he plunged deeper into his loss of it. He could not stand their company for more than an hour at a time.

Christmas Eve was especially painful. A stuffed goose and fig pudding feast with boisterous, wine-soaked relatives sank him to new levels of gloom. Retreating to a window in the Blue Room when the others moved the festivities to the larger drawing room, he stood quietly staring at the misted, lamplit view of London. How did Melody Bainbridge celebrate Christmas? he wondered. Did she think of him as often as he thought of her? Why had she disappeared? Why did she not return?

She was not sequestered in Hertfordshire with her cousin, Blanche. He had checked into that possibility himself. A long, cold ride to the cottage in the country, a day spent listening to Blanche's weepy concerns. "Where could dear Melody be? If she has not told you, and she has not informed me, in whom has she confided? You do not think Burke has gotten his hands on her, do you?"

"She had sent you no word? None at all?"

"Only this paltry thing." The paltry thing a note, in Melody's hand, postmarked from London. It begged Blanche not to worry.

"I am safe," it read, *"and in order to keep you equally safe from Burke who might punish you for harboring me, I mean to disappear for a while. I must think things through with regard to my future."*

"Are you all right, Dunstan?" It was Gillian who discovered him. She pushed aside the drapes to join him in the cool, dark alcove created by the bow window. Gillian, her face brightened by the spirits of the evening, the dark wings of her hair pulled back into a gleaming knot of braids. Gillian, his beautiful Gillian. Motherhood would seem to agree with her. She had not faded with the years. It was only the feelings between them that were dimmed.

"Too stuffed wi' goose and overheated by the wine," he lied. She invaded private territory. He found himself strangely reticent, unwilling to share intimacies with this, the woman he had once asked to be intimate with him for the rest of his life.

"But you ate little, drank less, and now you hide away from us."

"You would seem to have no trouble finding me."

"The Dunstan I once knew always liked to stand in windows."

"And you did always find me." The memory was unwelcome.

She bit her lip, chastened.

"I am little changed since then," he said. "Auld habits die hard."

"To the contrary. You seem greatly changed. Distracted. Distant."

"Am I? I suppose there is a difference. When last you found me here, my thoughts centered on nothing so much as stealing a bit of time alone with you. Today—"

"Today?"

"Today I am content to steal a bit of time alone with myself. Do forgive me, my mind is miles away."

"Yes. Of course." She fell silent, but only for a moment. Gillian had never cared for silence. "Is it Scotland you yearn for? Or perhaps a certain Lady Bainbridge?" She asked the question lightly, and yet he knew the nuance of her voice as well as she his moods. His answer was not lightly anticipated.

His tone, therefore, was as serious as the glance she

threw his way. "You could always read my moods too well, Gillian."

"Yes, I could at that." She smiled. He could see the baring of her teeth, dimly reflected in the pane. She stood quiet a moment before lightly touching his arm. "If there is anything I can do, Dunstan, should you ever wish to talk . . ."

"You would gladly hear me out," he suggested, his tone as chill as the night. "You are too kind." It was a dismissal.

She heard it as such, removed her hand, and backed away. "Yes. Well," she said uncomfortably, "I must see how the boys get on."

She dragged back the edge of the curtain, shedding light on the window, casting London into greater darkness.

It occurred to him to ask, "Why *did* you leave me, Jill?"

"Is it only now you think to ask me?" The curtain slipped from her fingers, shrouding them in gloom again.

He did not turn to look, could not face the truth he asked of her. The question should have long ago been voiced, long ago answered. He had to know now—now that another love turned her back on him.

"Why?" he pressed. "I loved you. You claimed to suffer similar pangs. There was certainly some indication o' feeling in the kisses we shared in just such a secluded nook as this. I have never asked, never begrudged you or Barnard the happiness you found together. You are happy, are you not?"

"Of course I am," she said—too quickly he thought.

"I would know now. Why did you choose to go?" Still he focused on the night, on her reflection, could not face the answer head-on.

She took her time in answering. He began to think she might not tell him, but at last the words were thrust between them, to hang awkwardly in the confined space they occupied. "You wanted me to be something I could not be."

"Did I?" It was not so much question as contradiction. Baffled, he stood a moment, pondering. All this time he had held his mother's interference to blame.

Gillian flung aside the curtain, stalking away with a sigh. He halted her progress at the door with the same two words, this time a question, gently insistent, genuinely intrigued. "Did I?"

"You did!" she cried, an unexpected anguish voiced. "You know you did. You loved—still love—Scotland more than I could. More than you loved me. The very wild emptiness of it you found beautiful."

"Still do."

"You hate London, the smell, the crowds, the traffic. I adore it. Sights. Activity. Theater. Shops. I grow distracted and melancholy in the countryside, especially the Highlands. I could not escape them fast enough. You were convinced you, and you alone, could fill my every need."

He knew not how to respond to such a claim.

"And your mother!"

"Aye, Mother."

"You knew she was dead set against the match."

"And chose to ignore her."

"I could not. She was too persistent in her objections. I felt . . . alone, Dunstan, as if you did not hear my fears, my concerns, even as I voiced them. It was as if because you dismissed them, they did not exist."

"And Barnard? He didna' dismiss your concerns?" He said it with growing comprehension. Pieces fell into place.

"Barnard is a good listener."

He laughed, reality flooding, filling an emptiness that had too long rung hollow.

"It is not funny," she said, her back up.

"No," he agreed. "I find humor no' in my callousness. That was unforgivable; I do beg your pardon."

Her lips parted in surprise.

"I am amused only in the fact it has taken me so long to perceive it."

She shrugged. Silence stretched again until she

asked haltingly, as if the words fit unwell her mouth. "Did you listen to this Lady Bainbridge's concerns? Her fears?"

He pondered the question, as he paced the room. Flinging back the drapery, he exposed the black velvet of the night. London glittered like a row of brilliants pinned upon it. A chill shook him. "Perhaps no'. I know I have asked her to be, to do, something she would no'. And now she has run from me. Is lost somewhere out there." He raised his palm to the misted surface of the pane, as if by so doing he might touch upon the answers he sought.

"I am sorry. I hope you find her. I wish I might tell you—" She cut herself short.

"What?" he asked, but when he turned, she was gone, her wish, whatever it might be, left unspoken.

It was wishful thinking, not ghosts, kept Melody awake. Memories of Dunstan Hay, his slow smile, lilting voice, of a night spent wrapped in his arms visited her in wisps, phantoms of memory. Nights became her enemy—loomed too large, too cold, too lonely. Days were less of a problem. There was much to keep her occupied, mind and body.

Christmas passed uneventfully, the significance of the season lost in a flurry of dust so thick it reminded her of sawdust and Tunbridge ware, and thus, again, of Dunstan Hay and her cousin, Blanche, whom she had yet to inform as to her whereabouts.

Kerchiefs guarding their hair, kerchiefs guarding their noses, she and Maddie set to work. Too long had the place been left shrouded. The furniture, slipcovered against the dust of decades, was not sufficiently protected from the damp. A pale bloom of mildew spotted every surface. Each piece must be unveiled, scrubbed, dusted, waxed, and recovered. The pieces that were not ruined she stored in a logical fashion, as far from moisture as was practical. Most everything that had been left in the upper rooms was beyond salvaging, as were draperies, bed hangings, a half dozen tapestries, and a painting or two.

It was in January she felt most keenly the manner in which the gatehouse was giving up its fight with the elements. Time and neglect had too long abused it. The stones were loose in their mortar. Wind whistled mournfully through many a chink. The roof leaked. The fireplaces smoked abominably. The very foundation of the walls seemed to shift. The masons and slaters she called upon to recommend what might be done shook their heads and told her the place was beyond saving.

Melody was loath to admit defeat. Too well she understood the desire to in some way preserve the glory that had been Byngate. She made additional inquiries into possible repairs.

In the first weeks of February, Melody, too long trapped in the damp misery of the gatehouse, too long obsessed with dust and mold, rotting timbers and crumbling mortar, wrapped herself in the comfort of her cloak and went out to walk among the fallen manor walls. Her ramblings did little to cheer her. Sadness gripped her to see a once fine structure reclaimed by nature's chaos. There was within the landscape of ruins a pointlessness to her efforts, a despair that harkened to the deepest layers of her soul.

In scaling the tumble of stone, in viewing the horizon by way of glassless windows, she was struck by their parallel to her own situation. Here stood her marriage personified. There was no hope for it, no way to repair damages done. A tragedy, that. Greater tragedy, perhaps, in regarding the gatehouse. It cut so solid a silhouette against the clouded sky. A pity it, too, was destined to crumble like her hope for a future with Dunstan Hay. The clouds misted rain upon her in keeping with her mood. Standing thus, among shattered dreams and ruined masonry, face lifted to the heavens, she wept, tears lost in the rain, hope at its lowest ebb.

With March came more rain, it poured from the

skies as if set on drowning them, the steady, pounding force of it dripping in on her and Maddie in a hundred places, plopping musically into a myriad of bowls, basin, pitchers, and tubs that had been placed on every available surface.

"There's no saving this," she said both aloud and in the letter she wrote to Barnard, recommending he decide how to dispose of the gatehouse's contents.

Maddie agreed, as if she had long since come to the same conclusion. "All our work for naught," she said.

"Nay!" The word popped unexpectedly from Melody's lips, and with it memory of the man who had so often used it. She shook her head, shook away the chilling melancholy that gripped her, as if the ghost of the woman in white had passed through her on her way to the window. "The furniture is saved, and the stones may be used for rebuilding. It is not wasted effort."

Maddie shrugged. "Yes, miss."

And so began the task of packing up what furniture was to be sent to Scotland, and arranging for its transport. Advertisements were run for the sale of much of it, the rest to be given away. Additional advertisements were run in the hopes a local mason would find use for the stone.

The weather warmed, the days running into weeks and then months of a dreary sameness. Like twin specters, Melody and Maddie moved through leaky, shrouded rooms in that ghost of a gatehouse, the space echoing more empty and desolate by the day. By night, lonelier still, Melody's mind all too alive with memories shoved aside in the fervor of her daily labors—she thought of Dunstan Hay.

In her bedchamber, a room in which she felt the cold more than anywhere else, despite a crackling fire and tapestry-lined walls, she poked high the blaze, warmed her goose down coverlet and flannel nightwear before it, and wrapped herself in the length of a woolen shawl. She must return to London soon. Knowing that, she circled her bed, reading, as she had read dozens of times before, the papers Dunstan had left on the mantel in London. These were the documents from the black-ribboned folio, papers now pinned to the brittle, age-raddled bedcurtain. Like Lady Anne of Knole, she would absorb the truth that dangled before her nose.

What was it possessed Dunstan to gather together this history of failed dreams, dashed hopes, and the loss of her innocence? Night after night she pondered the question. There was nothing here she had not seen before: her marriage settlements, the transfer of deed for Bainbridge Hall, a handful of canceled promissory notes, an accounting of Bainbridge debts vs. Bainbridge possessions, Mr. Whitfield's proposal of divorce, legal documents attesting to her abuse. The language was perfectly penned, stilted, and formal— at odds with her memory of raw, visceral violence.

The words swam in the firelight, their fascination for Dunstan as unclear to her as the deeply shadowed corners of the room. Her mind was resistant to their meaning, and yet she was convinced Dunstan saw something important in them.

In the process of pinning up the pages she found the note. A slip of paper, it fluttered from between the pages of the accounting ledger, a flat white kite that sailed toward the fireplace. She pounced on it before flame could claim it, a note scrawled in a hand to match that which had written *Gone to look for you* on the outside of the folio. Dunstan's hand. He had yet to find her.

"Scarlett," two tt's it read at the top, and then: "divorce *a vinculo matrimoni*" and "divorce *a mensa et thoro*." Beside the first phrase, at an angle, a single word followed by a question mark. "Fraud?"

Still confused, she climbed into the bed, behind the rustling curtains. What did "Scarlett" mean? A color misspelled? What fraud? And what had any of it to do with her divorce? Exhausted, she determined to read it all again tomorrow. The answers must be there. She would find them.

Snuffing the candle, she dove into the warm cocoon of bedding, settled her head on the pillow, tucked the folio Dunstan had scribbled upon beneath her pillow, and shut her eyes, fingertips touching the stiffness of leather-bound pasteboard. It was, of course, Dunstan she longed to touch, not this meager sample of his penmanship. *Gone to look for you.* Did he look for her still? Sleep lured her as her thoughts wound down, as the memory of her night in Dunstan's arms rose to comfort, to tease her. A thought, wispy as smoke, drifted across her consciousness, started her awake, sat her up in bed with a jerk. Mindless of the cold, she jumped from the covers, caught up the candle, and lit it by way of the fire.

The truth leapt out at her from every page now as she circled the bed. *Whitfield!* Whitfield would hear of this.

Simple words, a simple idea, so simple she doubted its power, and yet all made sense in this simplicity, all but the first word. *Scarlett?*

Melody chuckled as she read, puzzled by the one unsolved mystery. Amusement, astonishment, and rage welling, she clasped hand to her mouth, snorting her contempt of laws that valued property above a woman's safety. *The house.* Was her freedom trapped between real walls rather than symbolic ones?

Her laughter a long-needed release, she bent double, racked by a scathing outburst of noise, aching, tearful, derisive guffaws to think Whitfield so witless as to have missed what Dunstan had found. Hands to mouth, she fell onto the bed, heart overflowing with desperate noise, a wild, sobbing laughter so violent it frightened her. She muffled her panicked outpouring in her pillow.

She had abandoned hope, and now, unexpectedly, in a single word, it was returned to her.

Fraud.

Chapter Twenty-four

London, July 19, 1821

On Coronation Day Mr. Mason arrived on Lady Hay's doorstep, urgently demanding an interview in the very half hour Mr. Potsby had set aside for dressing Lord Hay.

"An unconscionably early hour for callers," Potsby opined as he finished shaving Dunstan.

"Mason is business," Dunstan corrected him, though his business, as yet, proved fruitless. Seven months Mason had failed in his search, seven months Dunstan had hovered in London, his affairs in Scotland tended from a distance, the delivery of the plants and bulbs he had taken such care to gather no longer important. His gardener handled the plantings, wrote itemized lists of what took root and what did not. He encouraged Dunstan not to fret over the cherry saplings that failed to flourish. Dunstan had room for only the one concern—Melody Bainbridge—and Mason had promised to find her, might have news even now kept waiting.

"Send him in, send him in." Dunstan grabbed up linen to dry his chin, as eagerly as he grabbed reason to hope from Mr. Mason's untimely call.

Potsby dared suggest, his tone subservient, "Might I take the liberty, my lord, to remind his lordship that Lady Hay will not be pleased if anything serves to delay your party's progress, this morning, of all mornings."

"Point taken, Potsby. Show him in."

"As you wish." With a far more distinguished air than Dunstan's unexpected guest possessed, Potsby ushered him in.

"You have found her?" Dunstan knew the answer before Mason ever opened his mouth. Defeat sagged in the wallpaper cheeks, took the starch out of Mason's wallpaper posture.

"No, sir. I am sorry. Still no sign of Lady Bainbridge. Something, rather, someone else. He may be able to shed some light on her whereabouts."

"He? Who? Be quick, man." Dunstan flung a freshly pressed shirt over his head and slipped his arms through the sleeves. "I would hear the whole of it, and have other obligations this morning."

"A Mr. Burns, sir. He was, until recently, in the employ of Lord Bainbridge."

Neckcloth next, well starched, an unwelcome restraint if this day proved as warm as the morning promised. He leaned into the cheval glass, fingers busy, his gaze darting to Mason and back again. Seven months she had disappeared without a trace, without a word. Seven months of hunting, of worrying, of a loneliness unlike any he had ever before experienced. "Bainbridge has her, has he?"

It was his greatest fear, the idea that she might be mistreated, and nothing he could do about it.

"No, sir. I have no evidence to that effect."

The cloth would not do as he wished. He stripped it impatiently from his throat, reached for another, and focused on the tying of it as he asked, "What is this Burns's business with Bainbridge? How can he help me?"

"Perhaps it would be best if he explained."

Again his fingers faltered. His gaze met Mason's in the glass. "He is here?"

"Yes. I took the chance—"

"Bring him in then." He forced the cloth into a presentable knot. Mason was at the door before Dunstan thought to ask, "This Burns. You say he left Bainbridge? Why? Is he to be trusted?"

Mason's expressionless calm was a strange comfort. "I believe so, sir. Unpaid, he was, for services rendered."

No surprise that. Bainbridge was up to his ears in debt. It would seem he owed every tradesman in London. Dunstan turned from the mirror, donned his waistcoat, and fastened the buttons, his attention fixed on the door.

The gentleman who followed Mason into the room was immediately familiar. Squat and portly, he had tobacco-stained teeth, a badly bewhiskered chin, and mittened fingers in which he clutched a battered brown cap. All that was missing was the cigar.

"I know you," Dunstan blurted. "From Tunbridge Wells!"

"We shall be late," Gillian said, dolefully wafting her fan as the carriage slowed to a snails' pace. To her nose she held, on occasion, a silver vinaigrette, exuding attar of roses, the faded essence of crushed petals holding at bay, if only for the briefest of moments, the reek of the Thames. Regret and a hint of petulance marred the roses of her mouth, her cheeks. Smoothing wrinkles from the heavy damask of her elaborate court costume, she complained of the heat, the stench, the delay.

Barnard, who drummed an impatient tattoo on a window that revealed nothing but the view of three more carriages come to a standstill, felt compelled to state the obvious. "The streets are mad with crowds."

"A dreadful press!" Lady Hay complained, her fan busy. "I cannot see how we shall ever get through it before the ceremony begins."

"My fault, not getting us off to an earlier start," Dunstan admitted distractedly, his mind as busy as the fly that futilely fought to force its way through the glass of the window.

"Who was the gentleman you were so long closeted away with?" his mother asked.

Dunstan stared blankly at the sea of sunlit faces lining the street side, not one of them the face he longed for.

"Two gentlemen—Mr. Mason and Mr. Burns." He had no wish to explain.

"And what business have this Mason and Burns that you should be bothered by them so early on this day, of all days?" Barnard asked.

"Information. They are gatherers of the stuff," Dunstan said, unprepared for the sudden swiveling of heads reflected in the window. Every face in the carriage, like flowers to the sun, bloomed in his direction.

"Information? What kind of information?" His mother's voice was shrill.

He glanced over his shoulder at them. Barnard looked decidedly nervous. He tugged at his neckcloth. Sweat beaded his upper lip. The transformation intrigued.

"All sorts." Dunstan said as he lowered his window, freeing the fly. In the glass, as it moved, he studied with growing interest the way Barnard's agitated gaze sought out his mother's.

What was going on?

The air in the coach seemed as pregnant with expectation as it was immediately fecund with the smell of dung and sweated horses and too many people gathered in the streets.

"Surprising what they can ferret out."

He turned to face them.

Gillian wore a guilty sort of curiosity along with her finery. "The third fellow who arrived in such a hurry?" She suggested the question rather than ask it outright.

"Mr. Scarlett. My solicitor," Dunstan explained.

Odd, that his mother felt the need to elaborate, saying, "Considered the best counsel in London."

As if this talk of Scarlett's credentials in some way concerned him, Barnard asked, "The same Scarlett who turned down Queen Caroline when she asked him to represent her before the House of Lords?"

"The very same." It was not Dunstan, but his mother who answered.

"What need of him have you?" Gillian asked, curiosity unabated.

Dunstan shrugged. "He is intrigued by Lady Bainbridge's case."

"Lady Bainbridge?" Again Barnard and his mother shared an exchange of unsettled glances, as if his words were stones thrown into the still pond of their concerns. "Does she not already employ a solicitor?"

"Whitfield! Incompetent fool." Dunstan spat out the words.

"What is wrong with this Whitfield?" His mother sounded irritable. That she should be interested confused Dunstan. That she should be irritated confounded him.

"Besides his being an ineffectual, boot-licking weasel?" he asked wryly.

"Is he ineffectual?" Gillian, squinting against the sun, plied her fan vigorously.

"Completely. And now that I discover he has been paid to serve Lord Bainbridge—perhaps better than Lady Bainbridge—the level of his incompetence makes perfect sense."

"No," his mother said.

"Is he?" Barnard would know.

"Oh dear," Gillian said, fan fluttering.

Glances again, worried ones, and all of them far more interested than Dunstan expected.

"To what purpose this ineptitude?" His mother delved the heart of the matter, and with her question an idea seeded in Dunstan's mind, a wild, unfounded notion he did not want to give growth, much less see bear fruit.

"Lady Bainbridge might long ago have been completely free of her husband if Whitfield had only pursued the matter of fraud," he said.

"Fraud? Was there fraud?" Her tone, their combined regard, would seem to indicate a vested interest in his reply.

Misgiving took root again. He answered warily. "Bainbridge Hall was listed as one of the assets Bainbridge brought to the marriage. Seems it was no longer his to offer. Bainbridge needed money to cover debts he did not make known."

"Remarkable," his mother said, her voice very low.

He nodded. "Ironic, too."

"Yes," Gillian agreed, her fan fallen lifeless in her lap. "That a woman may obtain her freedom because of fraud rather than because her husband beat her. Do you not find that ironic, Barnard?"

Barnard cleared his throat, uneasily fingering his neckcloth. "Life is all too ironic, is it not?"

Dunstan laughed wryly, testing his suspicions. "Ironic, indeed. I have stumbled upon the solution to Lady Bainbridge's troubles, but have no idea where to find her. There is some irony in that, I suppose."

Gillian blinked, then looked away. Barnard could not meet his gaze. Even his mother seemed suddenly preoccupied with the beading on her bodice.

Perceiving weakness in the uncomfortable silence, perhaps validation of his suspicions, Dunstan pressed on. "Melody Bainbridge would seem to have disappeared from the face of the earth."

The breathless stillness within the coach was disturbed by a cacophony of cries and catcalls without. A shrill whistle turned Gillian to the window. Boos and hisses dragged Barnard's attention from an inspection of the shine of his boots.

"The queen, the queen forever!"

Even Dunstan could not refrain from glancing toward the distraction of a street full of waving handkerchiefs.

"The queen," Gillian said uneasily, as drawn to the noisy drama without as she would seem to be discomforted by the quiet drama raging within. "No mistaking her bays. Also Lady Hood and Lady Hamilton with her."

"We shall not get any closer to Westminster if we remain in the carriage." Barnard had the manner of a creature trapped, a creature who would escape the uneasy tension hung thick in the coach. "Do you mind walking the rest of the way, my dear? Can you manage in that dress?"

Deep within Dunstan's heart, the sense of deception resonated. Not the first time these three had kept the affairs that touched his heart most keenly secret from him. The past repeated itself.

Gillian agreed she could manage quite well. What a splendid notion. Barnard leaned out of the window and called to Swan to stop. They meant to get out.

"Barnard," Dunstan said, low-voiced.

Barnard darted a look his way, quick, worried, desperate.

Rage rose like gall, a rage mixed with despair. Betrayed by those nearest and dearest. *Betrayed!* Dunstan grabbed a sleeve, even as his cousin flung wide the door. "Where is she?" he barked.

Barnard froze, rabbitlike.

"Oh, my dear. Do come!" Gillian cried from the street, escaped from the other side of the coach. "This is dreadful! They mean to lock her out!"

"Her?" Barnard blinked and turned away, more than willing to be distracted.

Dunstan felt like hitting him. With a great show of self-control, he refrained.

"Who?" Lady Hay exhibited annoyance.

Gillian peered up at them, as if confused by their strange pose, their immobility. "The queen. Who else?"

Shouts in the distance. The sound of a heavy door clanging shut. Heads turned in the surging crowd, all attention focusing on the doors to the Abbey, which were in the process of being closed, one after another, with desperate haste—slammed shut in the face of the queen.

"Come along." Barnard shook loose Dunstan's hold and leapt to the street, where he linked hands with his wife and set off for the Abbey.

Dunstan poised to follow.

"Dunstan," his mother said weakly.

In her voice Dunstan heard answer to his misgiving. He closed his eyes to it, to the awful, unbelievable truth. She knew! They all knew where she was! The enormity of their subterfuge, their betrayal, tightened the muscles in his jaw, dulled his ears to the growing noise of the crowd—cheering, jeering. Just such a battle of emotion waged within him.

Wounded, he jumped from the coach in pursuit of his cousin, shouting, "Damn it all, Barnard. You must tell me."

At his heels, surprisingly spry, his mother, shouting his name like a litany, "Dunstan. Wait! Dunstan. Do wait! Let me explain, Dunstan."

Through the gathering crowd they pushed like fox and hounds, stilled only by the greater hue and cry of those assembled in the doorway now shut and guarded by two beefy prizefighters.

Lord Hood was arguing with the doorkeeper, voice raised and red-faced. "I present to you your queen, man. Surely it is not necessary for her to have a ticket!"

The doorkeeper's back was straight, his manner similarly unbending. "Our orders are to admit no person without a peer's ticket," he stated.

Good God, Dunstan thought, slowing in his pursuit, unwillingly distracted. They could not mean to refuse the queen entry!

Lord Hood's color rose. In his temple a vein pulsed. "This is your queen," he repeated, as if the doorkeeper were an imbecile. "She is entitled to entry without such a form."

The queen, herself, addressed the man with an uneasy smile. "I am your queen. Will you not admit me?"

A fine sheen of sweat glazed the doorkeeper's brow. His attention slid uneasily from Hood to the queen and back again. The crowd around him began to voice opinion on the matter.

"Let her in," some bawled out.

"Go home," cried others.

The worst of it were the growing number of voices that called, "Back to Como!"

Dunstan sought some sign of Barnard, of Gillian. They were lost to him in the crowd.

"Back to Bergami!"

"Shame!" hissed from mouths on all sides, though whether such sentiment was directed at the queen, or the doorkeeper who kept her standing in the street, remained unclear.

The doorkeeper sweated profusely, shirt points wilting, though his every word emerged as starchy as his posture. "My orders are specific. I feel bound to obey them."

"Dear God. This is dreadful!"

His mother's voice in his ear, his mother's hand at his elbow, Dunstan nodded. "A disgrace to the crown."

The queen laughed, a nervous, brokenhearted sound.

That awkward attempt at levity reminded Dunstan too keenly of a day at the waters in Tunbridge Wells, the day he had first set eyes on another woman determine to laugh in the face of humiliation. Unable to bear the mortification of his monarch a moment longer, he pushed brusquely through the crowd and tapped Hood on the shoulder.

Confused, Hood turned, his eyes registering no recognition.

Dunstan took his hand, shook it, and in so doing, passed the man his ticket.

Hood looked for a moment confused. He stared blankly at the ticket. Understanding dawned. Smiling, he raised it and shook it in the doorkeeper's face. "I have a ticket!" he cried.

There were laughs from the crowd, murmurs of approval.

The doorkeeper could no longer look Hood in the eye. His gaze, instead, he concentrated somewhere above the heads of the restive crowd. "Then, my lord, we will let you pass upon producing it. It will let one person pass, but no more."

Triumphantly, Hood turned to the queen. "Will Your Majesty go in alone?"

Caroline took the ticket, looked about her uncertainly, her head nodding, the long black curls of the wig she favored bobbing at each overly rouged cheek. But before she could make good her intention, one of the Gold Staffs, glittering impressively in formal, state-occasion attire, squeezed his way between Lady Hamilton and the wall in order that he might momentously block access to the door with the insignificant width of his body.

A trifle breathless, he puffed importantly. "Madame, it is my duty to inform Your Majesty that there is no place for Your Majesty in the Royal Box."

The queen stared a moment at the ticket she held. The idea that it purchased only the right to sit cheek by jowl among her increasingly hostile subjects, in the gallery, high above the Lords, removed from the splendor that was to surround her husband, excluded from her rightful place at his side, omitted from the sumptuous feast, seemed for the first time to register.

Her dark eyes went moist. The pale, dimpled pudding of her chin wobbled. "I am sorry for it," she said unevenly, and when Hood tried to further press her case, she laughed, eyes glittering with unshed tears, the sound of her amusement as brittle as bone china. Taking his arm, she inquired, "How can I get my carriage?"

She was driven away, the top of her landau down, sunlight illuminating traces of moisture upon her cheeks. Even in this, her direst moment of mortification, she was exposed to jeers and hisses, catcalls and laughter.

"Poor woman." It was Lady Hay who spoke.

Dunstan turned to her, chagrined. At the top of the steps he caught sight of Gillian and Barnard slipping through the doors to the Abbey. "I cannot take you in,

Mother," he said apologetically. "I have lost my ticket."

"I know," she said, reaching up to pat his cheek, a gesture most uncharacteristic. "No matter," she said, a strange gleam in her eyes. "I am no longer in a mood to see the crowning of this king, who does all in his power to humiliate his queen. Too much of your father in such a man." Her voice seemed unusually subdued. "Take me home, Dunstan. Take me home. There is something I must tell you."

Chapter Twenty-five

Lulled into a state of some security that nothing else untoward or unexpected could this day reach out to snap him in the nose, Dunstan was not at all pleased that he and his mother should encounter yet another rude surprise in awaiting the coachman a street urchin sought on promise of a coin.

"Hay!" His voice smote Dunstan first, from behind, a hint of threat even in the single syllable. "And who is this with you? Not my wife, as I might have expected."

Burke Bainbridge's carefully voiced volume and inflection, turned heads on the thronged walkway. Crowds had clustered all morning in order to catch sight of the king. Those exalted few thousand who could afford entry to the spectacle, thus became spectacle themselves.

"Bainbridge." Dunstan inclined his head ever so slightly.

"Can this be your mother, my lord? But surely this woman is far too young?"

Lady Hay was wise to the mannerisms of her son. She faced Burke with no more pleasure than did Dunstan, demanding, "Who are you, sir, to make so personal a remark?"

"Burke Bainbridge, Lady Hay. Perhaps you have heard of me?"

Lady Hay raised her lorgnette for an eagle-eyed stare. "I have, sir, and little of it to your credit."

"Perhaps you will think more highly of me when

you discover my purpose in approaching you today is to grant your son his fondest wish."

"How so?" Dunstan was no less wary than before. This man was the type to dangle carrots only to jerk them away.

Burke smiled. How Dunstan hated the sight of it.

"I would tell you I am willing to accept your terms."

"Would you?" Dunstan was skeptical.

"Yes." Bainbridge smiled too broadly. From his coat pocket he pulled a familiar folio of documents. "With only two conditions."

"Conditions?" Still, Dunstan dared not hope, dared not trust this man's intent. "What would they be?"

"Nothing of consequence, really."

Nothing? Dunstan listened to the singsong cry of a vendor hawking sausages to the crowd, waiting for the something hidden in this man's nothing.

"The first condition is a money matter, nothing more."

Nothing again. Dunstan closed his eyes briefly and licked his lips. How much nothing could he stand?

"How much of a money matter?" he asked mildly, the very softness of his voice drawing his mother's attention away from Bainbridge for the moment.

"The sum mentioned should be doubled."

"What gall!" Lady Hay huffed.

Dunstan silenced her with a glance and asked, "The second condition?"

"Why, it is no more than that you must return my wife to me, no matter how soiled, until the papers are made final. I shall be assured they are the more hastily attended to as a result."

Return her to him? Could it be true Bainbridge had no more idea as to his wife's whereabouts than did he? Dunstan let the silence hang between them, considering the matter, saying at last, "Too rich for my blood, Bainbridge."

As if the matter were settled, unworthy of further discussion, Dunstan turned and walked away.

"What? You cannot be serious. Would you let misplaced frugality rob you of your heart's desire, Scot?"

Dunstan stopped, fought down a desire to strike the man, and turned, Melody's words like a refrain in his mind. *You will not beat a violent man by way of violence. He is too well versed in the matter.* He would use his brain to beat the man—a brain unclouded by rage, unhampered by a need for revenge, clear of purpose, clear of intent.

He laughed, forced the noise between his lips, forced his stance to assume a more relaxed pose. "I know you better than you think, Bainbridge."

"Do you?" Burke sneered.

"Aye." He nodded. "You see me as nothing more than a cash cow, do you not? The stupid Scot. He loves her. He will pay for that love. Will he not? You are willing to divorce your wife for the charge of brutality. It is a manly flaw, after all, and serves your purpose, in relieving you of any responsibility for her upkeep. But you would not lose all hold on her—not while you're convinced there is still money to be milked from me. Have I got it right?"

Bainbridge's smile soured. He had nothing to say.

Dunstan was not yet finished. "I am sorry to have ever offered you a single copper in exchange for the safekeeping of the finest woman I have ever had the privilege to encounter, your wife. But I am willing to make you a generous offer, a singular offer, never to be repeated. I will triple the original amount—"

"Dunstan, no!" his mother cried.

"Aye." Dunstan nodded at Burke, his gaze never so much as drifting to his distraught parent. "You heard me right, and it is more than you deserve. I would warn you, not one additional grote will you e'er have off o' me again, but I gi' it willingly if you will sign a statement agreeing that your marriage is void because it is based on fraudulent terms."

"Fraudulent terms?" Burke scoffed, a thread of fear in the fabric of his gaze. "What fraudulent terms?"

"Can you think o' none? I was convinced you were a clever man."

"Why should I so blacken my name?" Burke lowered his voice.

Dunstan's volume from the start had been circumspect. "Because that dirty name would then be freed to fasten to some other poor maid."

"And my wife might then be yours?" The words burst from him, heavy with sarcasm. All within hearing distance turned to stare, as was Bainbridge's intention.

Dunstan studied him, nonplussed. How did one deal with a man whose mind, whose motivations were so differently disposed? "That would be her decision," he said quietly. "But I have yet to hear your decision, sir."

Bainbridge studied him without response.

"Will you take the money and be satisfied? Refused, the offer no longer stands open to you."

Burke eyed him narrowly, as if weighing how serious was his intent. For an extended, hopeful moment, Dunstan believed him ready to acquiesce.

But no.

"You offend me, sir," Bainbridge said at last. "It is a pittance you offer. Ten times the amount is not enough to grant so great a favor, so great a freedom."

Dunstan nodded solemnly. He had hoped the answer would be otherwise, but found no great surprise in having been refused. "More than you deserve, sir. Far more than you deserve."

Turning, he took up his mother's arm and would have walked away at once had not Bainbridge raised his voice to demand, "Where is she, Hay? You cannot keep my wife hidden away from me forever. I shall have your head for it should you try."

That this man should ask relieved Dunstan's mind of the last vestiges of worry. His mother's hand, however, was shaking. He gave it a soothing pat before answering in all truthfulness, "Misplaced your wife, have you, my lord? Do you really think I'd be telling you her whereabouts if she does not see fit to do so herself?"

Chapter Twenty-six

London, August 11, 1821

He was on his way to Buckinghamshire at last, Melody's location revealed two weeks past by his mother, a detailed map drawn out for him by his cousin. Scarlett—a master at the law and all the proper documentation it entailed—had finished his business in locating exactly the evidence required to establish irrefutable grounds for a divorce *a vinculo matrimonii*. Copies of the documents filled a pouch Dunstan was to fetch on his way out of town at Scarlett's offices. All that was required at this point was Lord Bainbridge's signature, Lady Bainbridge's signature, and the approval of the court, and Melody was a woman freed of the confining bonds of matrimony, a woman free to follow her heart elsewhere. To Scotland, he was hoping.

Fresh horses in the traces, renewed hope surging just as spiritedly in his breast, Dunstan set out with every anticipation of a happy ending to this business of love. He did not anticipate a snarl in traffic. He did not anticipate the queen.

Unaware of any royal influence upon his fate, Dunstan exhibited limited patience when Swan was forced to stop the horses no more than a dozen paces from Scarlett's office.

"We've a day's hard ride ahead of us, man," he grumbled through the trap. "We shall never get there if you canna' so much as slip London. What is the delay?"

"The queen, sir."

"The queen is dead, man, three days and more."

"Precisely, milaird, and the dead move none too fast you'll be noticing."

The post coach in which Melody took passage, ran into traffic in Ludgate Hill, near St. Paul's, a long line of vehicles drawn to a dead standstill on both sides of the street. Teams without check-rein stood head down and hip-shot, as if they had been kept waiting for quite some time.

A lengthy bout of shouts sounded from above them before the postboy hopped down from his station above the boot and perched on the iron step rung, that he might peep in the window. "Funeral procession, folks. It will be a moment's delay. It is the queen, you see. Lord bless her. Word was this morning she was to travel by way of the Thames. Our whipster would have gone by another road, had we known a mob would block the way at Hammersmith."

"A mob? Are we in danger?" The young woman who sat beside Melody grabbed up her daughter in alarm.

"No danger, love. The crowds have only turned the funeral procession east into Temple Bar, that it should pass through the heart of London, rather than go around as the king requested."

The information passed in shocked whispers from mouth to mouth among the passengers inside and out. There were four, in addition to Melody, crowded inside the post coach: a polite, bewhiskered gentleman who introduced himself as a banker, an old woman with bright, blue eyes and a lap full of knitting, and a plump young mother, whose four-year-old daughter, red-cheeked and bouncy with curls, removed her thumb from her mouth every quarter of an hour, to ask plaintively, "Are we almost home, Mummy?"

The young woman nodded patiently as she had nodded many times in the course of the journey. "Almost home, my dear," though this time she added sadly, looking at the others suggestively, "just like the queen."

Melody, who knew nothing of the circumstances of Caroline's death, could not resist asking. "Is not England, then, home to its queen?"

"It is to Brunswick she returns," the gentleman banker informed her.

"We did never sufficiently make her welcome here," the old woman suggested darkly over the rhythmic click of her knitting needles.

"We did not," Melody agreed.

"I hear she went to Drury Lane the last time she was seen in public." The young woman whispered over her daughter's head. "Sick she was, and yet she would see the reenactment of the coronation since she had been turned away from the real one."

The banker broke in. "Like a portrait Elliston was."

"You were there?" The old woman tugged at her yarn and resumed counting her stitches.

"Yes. A performance not to be missed. So exactly did the man portray the king you might well have supposed the theater had become for the moment, Westminster. Perhaps the queen herself was confused. It was said she had dosed herself liberally with laudanum and medicants for the nerves. It is the only explanation in my mind for her having gotten up at the close of the performance, looking quite wild-eyed and haggard, to curtsy to the manager."

"Curtsy?" Melody interrupted, thinking back to the day she had curtsied to the queen in the rain.

"Yes. Curtsied to everyone she did—pit, galleries, boxes—her manner so insistent, so unexpected, the audience met her with no more than a smattering of applause."

"Poor daft creature," the old woman muttered.

"Indeed! There were any number of ladies, my own wife included, who burst into tears to see her so lowered before a house full of her subjects."

The young woman covered her daughter's ears to

whisper, "Dreadfully sick I hear she was that evening—vomiting and feverish."

The little girl shook her hands away and listened with an expression of uncomprehending consternation as the potbellied banker told them, "Her doctors declared it an obstruction of the bowel."

"She was b-l-e-d. Profusely." The young woman spelled out the horror.

The postboy leaned in the window to share in the discussion. "Dosed with opium and castor oil, she was."

"No castor oil," the little girl piped up.

"Not you, my dear. Someone else," her mother comforted.

"To no avail." The old woman snipped at her yarn and tied on a new thread. "Knew she was dying, she did. Told them as much."

"Her doctors thought they knew better, bloody fools!" The banker shook his head.

The old woman went on grimly. " 'I am going to die' she told anyone who would listen. 'But it does not signify.' "

Melody was moved. "Not signify? Did she really say so?"

Conversation ceased as nearby churchbells joined in the distant tolling. A ripple of cries, like the turning of leaves in a bit of wind, swept the street.

"She comes."

"The queen."

Then shushing noises. All conversation ceased. Gentlemen doffed their hats.

Melody's thoughts returned to Tunbridge Wells, to the moment when Dunstan Hay had first doffed his hat and bowed to her.

All chatter ceased, every face took on a sobered expression. Odd to see such a quiet, dour crowd when the sun smiled brightly from a clear sky. The coffin was crimson, blood bright, in the midst of funereal blacks: black horses, black plumes tossing, black carriages filled with mourners in black, and afoot, more blackness from hatband to boot tip. Lord Hood, Lady Anne Hamilton, Sir Robert Baker, Sir Robert Wilson, the Lord Mayor, aldermen and members of the City's Common Council, like flightless ravens they followed her.

"God bless the queen!" No shouts. The words were murmured.

"May she rest in peace!"

"Where is the king?" Melody asked the young mother beside her.

The woman shook her head sadly, gave a few tisks of her tongue, and whispered, "Gone to Ireland, he has. Might have turned back, too, before he crossed the Channel. Word was sent his wife was ill."

"He does not perform the office of husband with any great understanding of the role, does he?" the banker murmured.

Melody, who understood all too well such a husband, leaned out of the window, her gaze locked on the passage of the coffin, the last she would ever see of poor Caroline, for whom she felt such an affinity.

"Broke her heart, he did."

It was as the old woman spoke, Melody spied him—across the street, his face framed in the window of a carriage—head bared, his familiar profile unexpected and enormously heart-lifting—Dunstan Hay!

As if she touched him, his gaze drifted from the procession and met hers. They stared at one another, dazed.

The solemnity of his expression deepened. The hawklike cast of his countenance sharpened. With winged urgency he quit his coach, launching himself into the press of people in the street.

Melody smiled, eyes misting, touched to see him stymied in his progress to reach her by the flow of mourners solemnly following the coffin, a picture of undignified urgency in the midst of so much stately lethargy. She laughed. The unexpected sound of her joy in the midst of so much sorrow turned heads. It drew unwanted attention.

She did not notice, had eyes for nothing and no one but Dunstan. Her head was occupied with nothing but thoughts of reaching him.

Throwing open the door of the coach that she might plunge into the river of mourners flooding her side of the street, she was halted by a voice, all too familiar, not at all welcome.

"Lady Bainbridge! Where have you been hiding yourself, my pet?"

Terrifying in its unexpectedness, in its cloying sweetness, every hair on the nape of her neck rose. *Burke!* The odor of his cologne sent an involuntary shiver like a ghostly hand along her spine. He stood in the crowd beside the coach, gloved hand held out to her, his person as spotless and trim as she had once hoped his character might be. A new walking stick was tucked into the crook of his arm, black-lacquered, with a gold lion's head knob. All in black he was today, but for the chalky white of his shirt. The colors of grief suited him, if not the emotion. He looked more distinguished, more dangerous than ever—a black cat beckoning a canary.

"I have been quite desolate without you, my love," he drawled. "Do step down."

Panicked, so great her need to escape his influence, she did not think beyond reaching protection, and that protection needs be Dunstan. Ducking back into the coach, she scrambled over the legs of her fellow passengers, wrenched open the far door, and flung herself free. She tumbled into the subdued throng below.

The queen's cortege had passed. The street began to stir, the crowd to thin. Shopkeepers returned to their wares. Traffic moved in one direction, if not the other. Skirting wide the spot she had last seen her husband, she headed in the direction she had spied Dunstan crossing the street.

"My lady! What an unexpected pleasure!" It was Mr. Whitfield popped up without warning in her line of flight, shoulders bowed, glasses perched upon his quivering nose. A pinched, rough-coated mouse he looked. A dear little mouse, small champion of her cause. How strange that the queen's final passage should bring together so many men important to her future happiness, right here at the crossroads of Fleet and Farringdon!

"Mr. Whitfield," she exclaimed, relieved to find an ally so near to hand. "You received my letter? The documents I sent?"

His mouse-bright gaze slid sidelong.

"Why yes, my lady." He clasped his hands before him, wringing them one through the other, as if he would make laundry of them. "The papers were delivered."

"What did you think of them?"

"Well . . ."

"Of my proposal for a divorce *a vinculo matrimonii*? Is there not sufficient evidence of fraud?"

His mousy gaze slid beyond her, his features assuming an uneasy watchful stillness, as if he observed the approach of a barnyard mouser as if he would much rather make a dash for his hole than respond.

"They made for a most interesting read before I fed them into the fire." The dreaded drawl came from behind her, the words delivered politely, low-voiced and pleased. *Burke again!*

She could not believe her ears! Looked from Mr. Whitfield to her husband and back again.

"Dear God!" With the sensation that the ground fell out from beneath her feet, she fit the pieces together. These two worked in concert against her! For a moment it seemed as if she in some way left her body as much as Queen Caroline had leapt from her earthly shell. Dizzy, disoriented, frantic, she scanned the crowd seeking the safety of Dunstan's presence.

Instinct prompted her to flee, but Burke anticipated her intentions. With bruising strength he gripped her arm.

His unwanted claim on her, the unpleasant pressure of his palm, his fingers, his very will, provoked a welling of emotion in Melody. A culmination of history, this closing of his hand on her arm. Hard on the emotional heels of the queen's heart-broken demise, Melody was no longer willing to accept his ruthless, proprietary restraint. Heat welled deep in her solar plexus, swept in an unexpected rush from the pit of her gut to the tips of her fingers. Her heart, her pulse, raced with a force never before unleashed. Without forethought, without considering consequence, she balled up her fist, drew back her arm as if to loose a bow, and let fly her fist.

Smack in the middle of Burke's perfect face it sank home. The force of the blow jarred her to the shoulder and stung every nerve in hand, arm, and elbow. It bloodied her knuckles and bloodied his nose. Crimson stained the chalk white perfection of his shirt-front, splattered the crisp splendor of his lapel, dripped inelegantly from his chiseled nose. Blood painted his upper lip almost as brilliantly as shock painted his perfect features.

For a high, singing moment she was possessed of complete satisfaction. An intoxicating rush of exultation overrode the pain in her hand. For one brief and darkly shining moment she understood why her husband was seduced by his own power, his own potential for violence. In that moment the mirror turned. He saw the world through her eyes. She viewed the world through his.

The bull enraged, he swung to face her.

Violence begets violence. She had said as much to Dunstan Hay. It did not do to fight a violent man with the weapon in which he was far better versed. Rage gathered in his eyes, coalescing in the movement of his arm, his hand. He meant to backhand her across the face. She recognized the immediate prelude to violence all too well.

Arm upflung to block the blow, eyes closed, she staggered backward. A breeze of sudden movement, redolent with the scent of French milled soap and a cedary sandalwood. A smacking sound, flesh against flesh, and yet she remained unscathed. Her eyes flew wide to witness Burke's backhand caught in midswing, Dunstan Hay blocking all harm that might come to her.

At his side two men, one vaguely familiar, one in the blue and red of a Bow Street Runner.

"Arrest this man! For attempted assault!" Dunstan cried.

Rage undimmed, Burke growled dangerously, fought the hands that would restrain him.

"Bow Street Patrol," the uniformed man called out as they scuffled. "Best not to resist, sir."

"You!" Burke cried when the second man, a potbellied fellow, made a grab for him. "Burns! Unhand me! You work for me."

The one he called Burns said stoically, "I work, sir, for them as pays me."

They were too much for him. The Runner pinned his arms behind him, lacing them together with a leather thong. Bound but unbeaten, Burke straightened and managed to look and sound lordly even with bloodstained face, rumpled clothes, and wrists confined. "The woman is my wife, sir." He said it proudly, with authority. "I have every right to reprimand her impertinence."

"It is true, my lord." The Runner politely addressed Dunstan. "I cannot arrest him for assault as long as he is her rightful husband."

Melody laughed bitterly. "There is nothing in the least rightful about our relationship, or his need to do me violence."

Whitfield cleared his throat to interrupt. "Indeed, Lady Bainbridge, that is not entirely accurate. It is true that Lord Bainbridge has, by law, every right to chastise you as long as you are still bound by matrimony." He wrung his rodential hands as if it greatly pained him to so inform her.

"Your fault, that oversight, you unworthy little man," Dunstan suggested contemptuously. To the Runner he said, "There is question, as to the legality of Lord Bainbridge's claim of a lawful marriage. I have proof, documents, that the marriage settlements were based on fraudulent terms."

"Documents? Ha!" Burke scoffed. "And who will attest to the authenticity of said documents? Certainly not the lady's own solicitor, for he stands before us."

Whitfield held up his hands as if baffled, shook his head regretfully at Melody.

Dunstan's voice was gentle, his manner confident. "Ah, but you are mistaken in that, my lord. The lady's solicitor is a Mr. Scarlett. He has offices in this very street if you care to consult him."

"S-S-Scarlett?" Whitfield stammered.

"Perhaps you have heard o' him." Dunstan was not above making the man squirm.

"Lady Bainbridge?" Whitfield looked stricken. "Is this true?"

For an instant, Dunstan, too, wore a look of concern. His gaze met hers over the head of the unhappy solicitor. Melody understood the look. He wished her to back his claims of Scarlett's representation, though she had never so much as met the man.

She laughed. "Why such surprise, Mr. Whitfield? You better represent my husband's interests than you do my own. It is a good thing, think you not, that the documents you allowed my husband to destroy were only copies of the originals? Otherwise, Mr. Scarlett would have excellent grounds to lodge charges of duplicity against you as well as my husband."

"This is all nonsense," Burke blustered. "Release me, sir, or I shall have you up on charges."

The Runner ignored the bluff, scratched his jaw, and shot a look at Dunstan. "Best take him in on the fraud charge, sir. They will only release him otherwise."

"Excellent idea!" Dunstan said. "Only allow me to fetch my coach and the necessary documentation and we shall join you. My lady?" He offered his arm.

In the instant she took it, it occurred to Melody she had never looked upon a more welcome prospect.

This man offered so much more than the fabric of his
sleeve, the solid warmth of the arm within it. He offered her freedom from the greatest mistake of her
life. He offered her a fresh start. He offered her hope,
happiness, and love. So much did he offer, tears
briefly blurred her vision.

His gloved hand covered hers and gave it a
squeeze. "I must make a note never to cross you, my
lady. That is a neat right jab you've mastered." His
voice was low, intimate, his remark for her ears alone.

She laughed.

"Och. Too long have I missed that sound." His sigh
wrung her heart.

"I am sorry I did not, I could not tell you where . . ."

Soft, his finger to her lips, he stopped her rush of
apologies. "It is music I hear in your laughter, my
lady, Melody. It won my heart, it did, the very first
day that I heard it."

They had reached his waiting carriage; he cupped
her elbow that he might assist her in mounting the
carriage step. She paused on the step to gaze at him,
had almost forgotten how dear was his face, how gentle the curve of his lips, how infinite the love glowing
soft in his jasper green eyes. "Dunstan," she said, then
could say no more.

"I looked for you everywhere, lass." His voice
broke. "I thought sure you were lost to me forever."

"I was lost and now am found," she said, voice
aquaver, giving his arm a squeeze, fighting the tremor
of her chin.

"Will you come home wi' me, to Scotland?" His accent was thicker than usual, his eyes brighter.

She smiled at him, eyes misting with tears for the
love of this man. "I am home." The words caught in
her throat.

His gentle smile faded. "Never say so, lass! I canna'
abide this city."

A tear spilled. She let it fall. "As long as you are
near, I am home, Dunstan."

Solemn as the first day she had set eyes on him, he

leaned close, gently kissed away her tear, and whispered low, his voice thick with emotion. "Will you promise, lass, never to run away from home again?"

For answer, she flung her arms about his neck right there in the street and kissed him soundly.

Epilogue

The marriage of Lord and Lady Bainbridge dissolved by the courts, Lord Bainbridge found a new home in Australia. A rough, brash, sometimes violent country, it was to the penal colony there he was transported for his crime. Never again did he set foot in England.

The Morrell cherry tree did not survive the violence of the weather at Hay Hall, but the Duchess of Dorset proved right, after all. Lord Hay did find something that took root in Scotland as a result of his visit to Knole. Indeed, it blossomed and bore fruit. The boy was named George, in honor not of the king as so many did suppose, but of Georgianna, the dowager Countess of Hay, who asked Blanche to be her traveling companion whenever she went into Scotland to visit her grandson, George, her son, Dunstan, and his beloved wife, Melody.